"Highly entertaining action that keeps you turning pages! A great fast paced thriller that I read from cover to cover and would highly recommend. Interesting twists and plenty of action!"

AMAZON REVIEWER

"Loved the book, looking forward to continuing the series. I didn't want the book to end,"

AMAZON REVIEWER

"A thrilling novella with two neighbors, one being threatened and the other is an FBI Agent. A short book with a huge storyline, will keep you enthralled!"

GOODREADS REVIEWER

"Thoroughly enjoyed this novella, it has interesting characters and and exciting plot based on current issues of technology. For someone like me who has in interest in both computing and mysteries, this was a perfect book,"

AMAZON REVIEWER

A thriller of the modern times. How an email could bring so many problems in a person's life. A well written story, easy to read that makes you turn the pages to learn what happens in the end. It mixes crime, greed, love, friendship, betrayal and seems very much credible to happen in real life. Look forward to continue reading books by this author."

"Wonderful! I wanted to see what happens, the characters were interesting. I would highly recommend it. I am excited to read another of your books,"

"This is a fast paced, exciting and thrilling novella. Dan Friedman holds your attention right up to the surprising ending that will take your breath away,"

"... This begins a roller coaster ride through this novella that keeps you turning pages.. This book is so well put together, you glide through quickly and can't wait to see what happens in the end where you are surprised by how it ends and can't wait for the next book in the series!"

"An extremely well written novella, craftily written with strong characters. One of the best novellas I have read for a long time and didn't want to put it down. Well done Mr. Friedman for achieving so much in a short story,"

"Highly entertaining action that keeps you turning pages! A great fast paced thriller that I read from cover to cover and would highly recommend. Interesting twists and plenty of action!"

"a very contemporary kind of situation involving money, partnerships and trust that reads like a "cops and robbers" story that will pull you in and wring you out wondering....WTF just happened". If this is a "novella"...bring on the series! Highly recommended 5/5"

"Short suspenseful read that is sure to please... Twists and turns, great character background and engagement with an ending that is a total surprise. Get this now, you won't be sorry."

PRAISE FOR DON'T DARE TO DREAM

"One of the best crime novels I've read in ages, full of breathtaking twists and turns."

—WILLIAM BERNHARDT, NYT BEST-
SELLING AUTHOR

"When reading a good psychological thriller, I hold to a couple of mantras: "Trust no one," and "Believe nothing." Great advice for anyone planning to dive into Dan Friedman's immensely entertaining debut *Don't Dare to Dream*, a story in which almost nothing is as it seems.

Friedman has created a masterful braiding of truth and lies that's guaranteed to leave readers amazed and satisfied. A fine first outing for this talented author, and I predict new fans will be clamoring for more."

—WILLIAM KENT KRUEGER, NYT BEST-
SELLING & EDGAR AWARD WINNING
AUTHOR

"Read this! Kept me wondering what was going to happen all the way through.
Recommended!"

—AMAZON REVIEWER

"A brilliantly plotted and enthralling thriller, Don't Dare to Dream by Dan Friedman is a huge literary achievement for a debut novel, with sophisticated characters, a strong premise, and fascinating twists.

Dan Friedman doesn't just keep the reader riveted to the pages as they follow this emotionally-charged story but keeps them guessing as well from page to page... an emotionally rich story imbued with psychological depth.

A great read told in a smooth, irresistible voice. It kept me awake through the night."

—READERS' FAVORITE BOOK REVIEW

"Fast paced thriller. I read this book in 2 sittings, taking a break for sleep and work.

I love the way the author creates and builds the characters, makes you feel like you are sitting right next to them and are a part of their lives.

Highly recommend."

—GOODREADS REVIEWER

"With *Don't Dare to Dream* Dan Friedman hits the sweet spot between the paranoia of Hitchcock and Highsmith and the subtle fear bred by the uniquely American cult of self-help and motivational thinking.

Twisted and thrilling, you'll hate these characters one chapter and cheer for them the next.

Highly recommended."

—BRYON QUERTERMOUS, BOOK EDITOR
AND AUTHOR

"It's a great page-turner and would make a perfect vacation read."

—KEN DARROW, EDITOR

NEVER REPLY ALL

DAN FRIEDMAN

For my better half.
You're the best.
I love you.

PART 1
REPLY ALL

ONE

Emily Turing couldn't help but open the email, even though it wasn't intended for her.

Nicely done! She won't see it coming, it read.

They addressed it to her, but in response to another email, she hadn't written. The unknown sender had probably pushed Reply All unintentionally.

If the email had ended there, Emily would not have minded so much.

But it didn't.

It had another line:

Get rid of her.

————

Special Agent Bob Alexis parked in the underground parking lot and took the elevator to the fifth floor. He walked through the long corridor and entered his apartment.

"Anybody home?" he asked as he closed the door.

He put his gun in the safe he'd installed a few months after his daughter was born. When no one replied, he took a shower, got into bed, and fell asleep immediately.

The next thing he knew, Madison jumped on top of him.

"Daddy! Daddy! Wake up!" she yelled with her squeaky voice.

"What the—" He almost yelled, but when he saw his daughter he smiled and hugged her.

"Hi, honey."

He glanced at the clock next to his bed. He'd only slept for two hours.

He couldn't stop yawning.

"You promised you'd take me to see the new *Frozen* movie!"

"I did?"

"Yes!" She said.

"Okay. Okay." He tickled her until she asked him to stop. "Let me get up and I'll take you."

He saw his wife Lisa behind Madison, half smiling at him. "Nice of you to show up," she said and left the room.

Bob shook his head, rose, and got dressed.

At the theater, he bought Madison popcorn and a large soda. A few minutes after the movie started, he fell asleep in the comfortable recliner. He woke up an hour later to his own snoring, which made the whole theater laugh along with his daughter.

Bob and Lisa had come to this theater a few times when they first started dating. They would share a large soda, a big popcorn, and hold hands for most of the movie.

He missed those days.

"How was the movie, honey?" his wife asked when they returned.

"Ask Daddy. He fell asleep again. And when he snored, everybody laughed at him."

"They laughed *with* me, not *at* me." Bob smiled.

"Go wash your face and hands before dinner," Lisa said.

"I'm not hungry, Mommy."

"You ate popcorn again?"

Madison grinned.

"I told you not to buy her popcorn," Lisa said. "She doesn't eat dinner afterward."

"I couldn't say no to her," he said.

"*That's* the problem."

After Madison fell asleep, they sat on the couch in front of the TV, like they did most nights Bob was home.

"I can't live like this anymore," Lisa said without looking at him.

"What do you mean?" He looked at her, but her eyes were still on the TV.

"You're never home."

"It's my job. What do you want me to do? Quit?"

She remained silent.

"It pays the bills, I have to—"

"You don't have to do anything!" She turned to him. "You could have chosen a different job. Something that would let you be a father and a husband."

"Like what?"

"I don't know. High-tech or something?"

"You think they don't work all hours in high-tech? I know exactly—"

"They work nights?" She asked. "They leave their family for a few days at a time?"

Bob rose. "I'm serving my country! I'm doing this so my daughter—our daughter—can live in a better world."

"Bullshit! You're doing this for your own ego. For the thrill."

"That's not fair."

"You know what's not fair? You leaving me here alone, day in and day out, having to raise her by myself. I've decided I can't stand—"

"Mommy? What's going on?"

They both turned to Madison, standing in the hallway. She rubbed her eyes and yawned.

"Go back to bed, honey." They both rose, but she gestured for Bob to sit down. Lisa led Madison back to her room.

He didn't know how much time had passed, but she startled him awake when she returned.

"And when you're home, you spoil her too much."

Did she notice I fell asleep?

Did she care?

"If you're awake." She sat on the couch, far from him.

"What?" He rubbed his neck.

"How many times do I need to tell you not to buy her popcorn before dinner?"

"You know I can't say no to her. Especially when I'm not around enough—"

"That's exactly the problem!" She rose.

He looked toward Madison's room.

"She's asleep. I had to sit next to her until she fell back to sleep."

"What's—"

"I do it almost every night. Not that *you'd* know."

He stared at the floor, which he knew his wife had wiped clean earlier. As she did every day.

He rose and held her hand. "I'll ask for an office job. Okay? I'll come home every day at a normal hour. Okay?"

She stared at him for a long time.

"It's too late."

"What do you mean?"

"I want a divorce."

TWO

Emily peered through the peephole and saw her neighbor, Bob, passing by her apartment.

Should I talk to him now? She held the door handle down, but couldn't bring herself to open it.

They said hello every time they met in the elevator. The second time they saw each other, Emily noticed Bob had a gun.

"Don't worry, I'm an FBI agent," Bob had said and smiled.

Emily smiled back, liking the fact she had an agent next door.

She saw the agent enter his apartment and decided she needed more time to think about what had happened. She thought of the email she'd received earlier. Emily emailed her boss about the problem she had found. Her boss replied. Emily had not liked her reply, but before she could understand what was going on, someone else—who Emily had never heard of before—replied to both of them.

Emily launched her email app and opened it.

Nicely done! She won't see it coming.

Get rid of her.

The original email Emily sent to Jessica showed discrepancies she'd found between the company's bank account and reports. Nothing strange or inconsistent with her job. Why would anyone be mad at this?

Emily wondered who had sent the email. The address it came from was a combination of letters and numbers, not a real name. Jessica, Emily's boss, must have sent Emily the first reply, as well as to someone else, but she put him or her in BCC, which meant Emily couldn't see it.

But when the third party sent a reply to Jessica, he accidentally pressed Reply All, so Emily received the email as well.

The threat.

Was it a threat?

What did it mean?

Should I involve the agent? Could he help me? Will he take it seriously?

Maybe I should wait?

Maybe it didn't mean anything?

Emily was always careful when replying to emails. Her greatest fear was to email the wrong person. It had happened once to one of their potential clients, who mistakenly sent them an email they'd meant to send to a competitor.

They had laughed for a long time in the office.

When Emily was a little girl, her father had taught her mother how to use email. He worked as an IT guy, but her mother didn't know much about technology.

"Never Reply All," he told her mother. "Always double-check who you send your email to."

Even though Emily probably knew more than him about computers by now, it stuck with her.

Now someone else had made the mistake, but it was her problem.

She had noticed the agent wasn't home much, and when he was home, he looked like someone who hadn't slept for a week. Emily would see his wife and daughter a lot. The wife seemed friendly and was good-looking. Emily wondered every now and then if they'd break up. Bob was nice and handsome—he even reminded her a little of Brad Pitt—but he was too old for her. Besides, Emily would never mess with someone else's husband.

———

Bob had met his wife late in life. He didn't talk much to women. He was only interested in his studies and in his job at the FBI. He wanted to save the world. As he got older, he realized the world could not be saved, but doing something to make it a better place was good enough.

He had first seen Lisa in a bar. He went there with his partner Craig after solving a tough case. He noticed her from across the room, sitting with a girlfriend.

"I think she likes you," Craig said.

"Nah." Bob sipped his beer, looking anywhere but at her.

"She's looking this way."

"Probably at you."

Craig laughed. "I don't think so."

Bob looked at her again. She seemed to be looking back at him.

She smiled.

Bob lowered his eyes. "She's probably bored."

"You'll never find another woman like that."

"I know."

"Go up to her and say something."

Bob shrugged. "Maybe later."

Craig shook his head. "You want me to go? I can talk to her for you. She's hot."

"No. That's okay."

When Craig got up to go to the restroom a few minutes later, Bob saw him stop next to her, whisper something in her ear, then point at Bob.

Bob shook his head at him.

I wish I could shoot him.

But she smiled and nodded her head. She wrote something on a napkin and gave it to Craig, who didn't go to the restroom. He came back and handed Bob the note.

"She wants you to call her." Craig sat down. "And I want to dance at your wedding. If you don't call her, I swear to God I'll kill you and claim self-defense."

———

"Did you call the pretty lady from the bar?" Craig had asked Bob a few days later.

Bob shook his head.

"Oh my God." Craig picked up Bob's desk phone.

"What are you doing?" Bob asked.

"I knew you might not call her, so I memorized her number."

"You *what*?"

Craig had an amazing memory. He would hardly take notes when they interrogated someone, while Bob scribbled everything down.

"I knew I couldn't trust you." Craig dialed a number, asked her if she remembered them, then handed Bob the phone.

A year later, Craig danced at their wedding.

———

Emily didn't know what to do about the email. She considered ignoring it. When she got to work the following day, she greeted everybody in the company, including Jessica, as if nothing had happened.

"Emily?" Jessica said. "Can you step into my office, please?"

That's it. She'll fire me.

Or worse, she'll tell me someone wants to kill me.

But who?

Emily ambled into Jessica's office, which was the biggest, filled with better furniture, and had an amazing view of Lower Manhattan. Emily had daydreamed about taking her place but knew she didn't have a chance. Jessica would never give up her seat, and they probably didn't value Emily enough to take her place.

Besides, Emily enjoyed working with her.

Jessica had launched the company three years earlier. She had used her own money and skills to develop a new technology, which helped businesses find their audience easily on social media. There were other start-ups which offered something similar, but Jessica had developed an algorithm which also helped companies know how their audience felt about their products.

They met at a meet-up in Manhattan, where all the participants were looking for co-founders. They had a long conversation which led to a few other meetings. They discussed the option of working together, even though Emily had little experience.

"I believe in you," Jessica said. "I think we would work

well together. You complete me. I don't believe in having a partner who agrees with me all the time."

Emily thought working with a woman would feel good. Would feel right.

Would feel safe.

Jessica told her how hard it was to find investors. She met many, but all of them turned her down.

"It's because I'm a blonde woman," she told Emily after a few meetings.

"Blonde?"

"Because I'm a *woman.*"

Emily considered. "Maybe you need to partner with a man. Maybe it'll make it easier for you to find an investor and—"

"Are you crazy?" Jessica rose in the middle of Starbucks. "If that's your attitude, I don't want you as my partner."

Even though Jessica had deeply insulted Emily, she knew she was right.

I'm sorry. I was wrong. We need to empower women at any cost. Emily texted Jessica a few days later. *If you still want me, I'll do everything I can to make the company successful.*

After a while Jessica replied, *Let's do this!*

A few months later they found an investor who believed in the technology. And them.

Before the investment, Emily worked for free, but received a small percentage of the company. She figured she needed the experience. She also believed the company had a lot of potential, and could be sold one day for a lot of money. She loved the idea she could be rich.

Even though Emily was the money expert, they made strategic decisions together.

Jessica held the door open for Emily, showed her in,

peered outside the office, and closed the door. "Have a seat, please." Jessica gestured Emily to sit down, walked behind her big desk, and sat in her executive leather chair.

Emily crossed her legs to hide her shaking knees and looked around. Like the rest of the offices in the company, Jessica's also had glass walls. It meant anyone in the office could see them.

"How long have you been the CFO of the company?" Jessica asked.

Emily raised her eyebrows. "Two years. A few months before we raised any money. But you know that."

"I do." Jessica rubbed her chin. "And how do you like working here?"

"Very much. Why?"

Jessica played with a pen from her desk. Emily couldn't help imagining it being a knife.

"Do you remember the documents you sent me?"

Does she know I know about the threat in the email? If she checked again, she could see the email was forwarded to me as well.

"Yes. Why?"

Jessica looked outside the office through the glass. Emily followed her gaze but saw nothing unusual.

"Am I being fired?" She almost rose in her seat.

"*Fired*? No. You're not fired at all."

Emily was a partner, but far from being an equal one. And the job title gave Jessica the option to fire her whenever she wanted.

"What's going on, Jessica?"

Jessica looked at her computer screen, hidden from Emily. "I think it may have been a misunderstanding. I double-checked the numbers, and I think they're fine."

Emily shook her head. "I checked those numbers a

million times before I came to you. You know me, I don't get my numbers wrong."

Jessica nodded. She turned the screen so Emily could view it. The company's bank account was open.

"You see? We have four hundred thousand dollars in the account. Nothing got stolen. You've got nothing to worry about."

Emily's mouth opened.

The previous day, the balance had been almost zero.

"It doesn't make sense, I—"

"It must have been a misunderstanding. Maybe they transferred the money or something." Jessica's phone dinged. She glanced at it and rose from her chair. "Or maybe it was a computer glitch. Or maybe a problem with the bank's computers. Anyway, it was solved. No worries." Jessica grinned. "I'm sorry but I have a call I need to make. That'll be all."

Emily noticed Jessica's face had turned white.

Should I tell her about the Reply All email I received?
Does she know I received it as well?

Something didn't feel right, so she kept it to herself.

For now.

Emily rose, thanked Jessica, and left the office.

A man almost ran into her as she closed the door. He didn't apologize or even acknowledge Emily. She'd never seen him and figured he came to meet Jessica, which happened often.

But the man walked toward the reception area and left the office.

Maybe a maintenance guy?

Emily entered her office, sat in her chair, and stared at the wall.

Mike, the VP of marketing who had the office next to

hers, stood outside her door and waved at her through the see-through glass. She gestured him in.

"What's wrong with your computer?" he asked.

"What do you mean?"

"Someone worked on your computer. He said he was an IT guy who came to fix it."

"What? There was nothing wrong—" She stared at her computer. "Why didn't you get me? I should call the police!"

"What do you mean?"

She rose. "We had an unauthorized person going through my computer!"

"*Unauthorized*? I don't think so. Jessica let him in herself."

THREE

"Divorce?" Bob's hands were shaking. "Why? We can work on our problems. We can go to therapy and—"

"We did *that* for a year," Lisa said. "The only thing it helped was the therapist's bank account."

He wanted to smile but couldn't.

They'd gone to therapy almost every week for a year. It cost them a fortune. The therapist seemed nice, but she didn't help them. Lisa always felt she'd taken Bob's side. Bob didn't want to agree with Lisa, but felt the therapist leaned toward his opinions.

But it didn't help their marriage.

"Can we think about it? Why rush? We have Madison to think about."

"We do. And I think it's best for her."

"To have divorced parents?" Bob's mouth opened wide. "Your parents divorced when you were young, and you always told me you hated growing up like that. You were mad at both of them."

She lowered her eyes.

She'd spoken about her parents a lot. She said she'd felt

17

alone growing up. She was jealous of Bob, since his parents were still together at seventy and seemed happy.

"Let's give it another shot." Bob blinked rapidly. "Please? For me? For *Madison*?"

"I'm sorry but I don't love you anymore."

———

Emily rose to go to Jessica but froze. She sat back and stared at her computer. Nothing seemed out of place. She looked at her files, shortcuts, and even ran a virus scan—but couldn't find anything wrong.

"Are you okay?" Mike stared down at her. She'd almost forgotten he was there. "Do you want me to get Jessica?"

"No. No." She shook her head. "It's fine. Probably maintenance I forgot about."

Mike nodded slowly. "Are you sure? You're pale."

She stared at him. Almost *through* him.

His new haircut she'd liked so much an hour ago was almost unnoticeable.

"I'm...fine." She tried to smile.

He nodded. "I'll be in my office if you need anything."

I could use a hug, she wanted to say, but it was inappropriate.

She'd hoped Mike would ask her out for a long time. Almost since he'd started working there. Even though she was a co-founder, they were both at the same level. Both vice-presidents, so there shouldn't be a problem for them to go out. Even though Mike seemed to be interested, he'd never asked her out. She tried dropping hints, but it never worked. Mike was too shy to do anything.

Emily had decided she wouldn't wait for him. She'd planned to ask him out at the end of the day, but now her mind went elsewhere. She'd been planning to ask him out for the past month. She had many excuses for why she delayed it. None of them had to do with the fact she was a woman.

She'd even asked Jessica if it was okay to ask him out.

Jessica had burst out laughing.

"I knew you had a crush on him!" Jessica said.

Emily swallowed. *I should have never asked her.*

"Don't worry about it. You should go get him." Jessica winked. "He's hot. If I weren't so busy, I'd do him myself."

Emily hated that kind of talk but knew Jessica was trying to compliment her. Jessica couldn't care less about being politically correct. Maybe that's what made her a CEO. She didn't care much about anything. If Jessica had been a man—she could probably lose her job over talking like that.

Emily both liked and hated that about her. Jessica could yell, laugh, make fun of someone, be funny and upset—all at the same time. Emily had hoped someone would sue Jessica, and Emily would have to step up and take her position.

Even though she wasn't sure she could.

Maybe she and Mike could co-CEO the start-up?

Even Jessica's approval to ask Mike out didn't push Emily hard enough. She had fair success with men, but nothing too grand. She didn't know if Mike liked her or not. He was nice to her, and they were good friends.

But he was also nice to others at the office, so maybe he was simply a nice person?

She could use someone to hug today.

She watched Mike leave her office and she returned to her computer. She searched her emails, but at first, found nothing wrong. When she searched for the email she'd received by mistake, she couldn't find it.

The last email was from Jessica. She couldn't find the Reply All email.

Someone had erased it.

———

Emily wanted to talk to Jessica about the missing email, but she'd never told her about the email to begin with. Did the man who came to her office erase it? Mike had said the man worked on her computer. He'd said Jessica gave him access.

Is Jessica in on it?

The email was intended for Jessica, so she must have been.

But Jessica didn't fire her.

Is it the other kind of 'get rid of me'? The terrible kind?

Emily kept searching for the email. It wasn't in her Trash folder. She searched online to see if she could recover permanently deleted emails. She discovered the admin could recover it within twenty-five days of deletion.

It would have been good news if Jessica hadn't been the admin.

———

Emily left the office earlier than usual. She didn't say goodbye to anyone and walked straight to the subway, blasting her ears with music from her AirPods.

Could I have been wrong? Maybe I only imagined this?

Maybe there was never such an email?

On the way home, she stumbled into a man looking upward.

"I'm sorry."

She drew back and took out one of her AirPods.

"It's okay," the older man said. "I've been trying to get this cat to stop howling. I live across from here, and it kept me awake all night long."

She looked up at the tree and saw a kitten watching her.

"He's so cute." She smiled.

"You like cats?" the older man asked.

"I like animals."

"Good. Can you get it to stop?"

"I can try," she said, but the man had already left.

When she got closer, she noticed a bad infection in the cat's left eye.

"You poor little thing," she said.

She wanted to call someone but didn't know who. She searched online and found the best way to catch a cat was with a blanket. She went home to find a blanket. She returned and climbed the tree. When she tried to grab the cat, she almost fell.

She walked with the cat wrapped in the blanket, trying to calm it down by stroking it, but then it scratched her from within the blanket. She almost let it go but figured it was just scared.

She took the cat to a nearby veterinarian she found online, who gave her an ointment for the cat's eye. She thought they'd take care of a stray cat for free, but they asked her to pay for it.

"I don't even know you, and you're costing me money, little kitten," she said.

They loaned her a cat box to take it home after she bought food and two bowls.

When she reached her apartment, she stared at the agent's door. She wondered if she should knock on it and ask for help.

Help with what? I have no proof.

Maybe the FBI can recover the missing email?

They'd probably need a search warrant, but she didn't think they had enough of a reason for that. Someone had returned the missing money to the bank account and had deleted the email.

The evidence was gone.

She put the bowls in the kitchen, poured food into one and water into the other. The cat ate most of the food and drank some water.

She couldn't keep her eyes off the cat.

She put the box next to the door, so she'd remember to return it. She'd promised she would take care of the cat and find a good home for it.

But after she named it Romeo, she ended up keeping him.

———

After five beers in front of the TV, she began thinking she was overreacting and reading too much into things.

Maybe I want to replace Jessica a little too much?

FOUR

Bob walked home from the office. He needed to think. What would he do alone? Without Lisa? How often he would be able to see Madison?

He wasn't ready for this.

It wasn't late, but he noticed a young couple sleeping on cardboard next to a Walgreens window. The man had no shirt on, showing his exposed ribs, covered only by the woman's arm.

It wasn't warm enough to be shirtless.

When he noticed he'd stopped to stare at them, he reached in his pocket and put all the change he could find in an old used cup next to them. Bob shook his head and continued home.

When he entered their apartment, Lisa greeted him with a soft 'hello' and went to their bedroom.

He took his shoes off and laid on the couch.

They hadn't decided on their sleeping arrangements, but he figured she needed the distance.

She also had said nothing about how she wanted the divorce process to advance.

He grabbed the blanket Lisa liked and covered himself. He laid his head on a throw pillow she'd picked up a few months before from Target.

He remembered the pillow fights they used to have when they were a young couple.

After two hours of staring at the dark ceiling, he decided he needed to do something else. He texted Craig at two a.m. to see if he could go out for a drink.

Craig never turned off his phone and hardly slept. At night, Bob used to keep his phone on vibrate mode, but when Lisa got upset it woke her up one night, he kept it on silent and would wake up every few hours to check it. And then went to the bathroom.

Working tonight. Sorry, Craig replied to his text immediately.

Bob wanted to ask what he was working on, but he didn't care. He grabbed a coat and went out.

He hated going out without his gun, but he knew he couldn't get drunk if he had it with him. It was safer locked up. He took a taxi to Manhattan and had the driver drop him off in front of the first bar he found.

He had a few beers and watched sports on TV.

"Great game, huh?" a man next to him at the bar asked.

Bob just nodded and said nothing. After a while, the man gave up and left.

When he returned home the following morning, Lisa and Madison had already gone out. He noticed Lisa never called or texted him to learn his whereabouts or to see if he was okay.

He called in sick for the first time in years, took a shower, and went to bed.

———

"You wanted to see me?" Emily entered Jessica's office at the end of a long day.

Jessica grinned. "I have some great news for you, my friend!"

Emily raised her eyebrows.

"A raise?"

Jessica shook her head. "Close the door. Have a seat."

"This can't be good."

"There's a conference I want you to go to. In Las Vegas. Next week. Three days." Jessica grinned from her big leather chair. "You up for that?"

"Yeah. Sure. In my field?"

"Dunno. Something about marketing and start-ups."

Why does she want me to go to something like that? Does she want to give me a bonus or does she want me out of the office?

"Marketing? Shouldn't you send Mike?" Emily asked.

"That's the fun part." Jessica kept grinning. "He's going as well."

Emily's mouth opened. "What?"

"Don't say I'm not a good boss."

"I didn't. But is this...does it make sense? I mean, financially?"

"You and your financials. I'm the CEO, remember? I want you two to go. *Together*. I need you out of the office. I need you to take a breather, learn new stuff. It's legal."

"I know it's legal, but it's—"

"Enough with that. I already bought the tickets. I'll forgo one of my trips. It'll balance your sheets."

Emily smiled. "Is it ethical?"

"To send the two of you?"

Emily nodded.

"Why wouldn't it be?"

"You know how I feel about him."

"Don't worry about it. You'll have two rooms, like any kind of company travel. There's nothing wrong with that."

Emily stared at her.

"Besides, I asked him before I asked you, and he said he'd love to go," Jessica said. "If you guys stay after the conference for the weekend, it's up to you."

———

Emily and Mike flew to Las Vegas the following Wednesday from JFK.

They didn't talk much during the flight. Emily didn't feel comfortable about the trip, knowing Jessica had fixed it up so they could be together. Emily had texted her that maybe they should call it off.

If you do, I'll fire you, Jessica texted back.

Then added a smiley.

Emily wanted to go. She could have only dreamed of having alone time with Mike away from the office. It didn't seem to bother him they were both going to an unnecessary conference.

Why would he mind? He's a man.

"Why do you think she sent you?" he asked before they landed.

"What?"

"It's marketing. Not financials."

"Right. Umm..."

"I think she wanted to hook us up," he said.

Emily swallowed hard. "Why would you think that?"

"We both know her. And we both know it's not your type of conference."

"I don't know." She bounced her knee.

Mike smiled. "Come on. She's your friend. She must have said something."

Emily blinked fast but said nothing.

"It's okay," he said after a while and smiled. "I like it."

———

They stayed at the hotel on the edge of town where the conference took place, so they couldn't walk anywhere. After they settled in their rooms, they took an Uber to a restaurant on The Strip.

The fact that Mike suspected Emily wasn't supposed to go to this conference could have meant he knew she liked him. If he did, and he agreed to go anyway—that was a good thing.

Maybe he wanted alone time with me as well?

On the other hand, why would he mind? Maybe he wanted to get lucky.

"Wine?" he asked her.

"You trying to get me drunk?"

"What? No! I—"

"Relax! I was kidding."

"Oh."

"I'd love some wine," she said. "Let's try the most expensive one. We have the company's credit card."

"We can't spend money for no reason. It's—"

She burst out laughing and held his wrist.

He blushed.

"Jesus! I thought the VP of Marketing would be less tight than the CFO."

He seemed more nervous than she was.

But he smiled.

She smiled back.

After one glass, she asked him how he got his job.

"I thought you were part of the decision process. Weren't you?"

Emily sighed. "She doesn't involve me in everything she does."

Mike nodded. "I sent my CV to Jessica right before I finished grad school. She interviewed me a couple of times and hired me. She said I'd have a lot to learn, but she trusted I could do it."

"That's great. She took me on with little experience as well. She's great."

"Yeah. She likes to give people a break."

She considered telling him about the email but decided he might make fun of her.

"Where do you see yourself after this job?" he asked. "I mean after we sell the company and you make a lot of money."

They smiled.

"I haven't given it much thought. I like where I am now. You?"

"I want to run my own company one day. I like the entrepreneurial part."

Emily nodded.

"Where do you see yourself family-wise?"

He raised his eyebrows. "I'd love to have kids. Maybe move to Jersey in a few years. You?"

"Nah. I'm staying in New York. Not even sure I want kids."

She regretted the question.

They had a full bottle of wine together, which affected her coherence. When they reached her room at the hotel, she asked him if he wanted to come in.

She couldn't believe she'd said that.

She wanted that more than anything.

But she was drunk.

And they were coworkers, on a work trip.

It would be all wrong.

"Maybe some other time?" he said.

"You don't find me attractive?"

Who said that?

"No. No. I do...but you...we drank too much. I can't. You'll hate me in the morning."

"I won't. But I understand." She nodded. "And I'll respect you for it in the morning."

The next morning, they dressed up nicely and went to the conference.

"I'm sorry about last night," she said as they waited for the elevator.

"What happened last night?"

She swallowed hard.

He doesn't remember? Was he too drunk?

I should have let it go.

But he smiled.

He remembered.

"It's okay," he said as they took the elevator down. "We were both too drunk. Besides, what happens in Vegas..."

She smiled.

At the conference, whenever he talked to other women, she felt a tingle in her stomach.

Not a good one.

It's nothing. He's being friendly. That's his job.

When they went to dinner, Mike suggested wine.

"Company credit card and all." He smiled.

"Look at you, spending the company's money. I'll tell Jessica about you."

"No. I—"

She laughed.

He joined her.

"Was that a 'yes'?"

She shook her head. "No wine tonight."

"Why not?"

"I want to be sober when I ask you to come to my room."

FIVE

Bob smiled as he watched Madison go down the slide in their apartment building's playground. He wished he had more quality time with her. He couldn't remember the last time he'd come home early in the afternoon and could play with her. She laughed as she came down the slide and melted his heart.

She waved at him and he blew her a kiss.

His phone dinged and he couldn't resist checking the message.

How is Madison? Lisa asked.

He sent her a picture of Madison smiling and waving, which got him a heart emoji from Lisa.

The heart was for Madison, not for him. It had been a long time since he'd gotten a heart from her. It had been a long time since she'd asked him how *he* was doing.

How are you doing? He texted back.

Fine. Thank you, she wrote back.

He put the phone back in his pocket and watched most of the other parents not taking their eyes off their smartphones while their kids played. He didn't have enough time with Madison to waste it on his phone.

Madison ate a snack next to him on the bench.

"Can I have a bite of your Oreo cookies?" he asked.

She drew them back. "Nah." She gave him a naughty grin.

"*Please?*"

She shook her head, and he pretended to cry.

"Okay. Okay. Don't cry." She broke off the smallest piece of cookie she could and gave it to him.

He ate it and then tickled her.

"Daddy?" she asked after a while. "Are you a good agent?"

"What?"

She stared at him.

"What do you mean?" he asked.

"Do you catch bad guys?"

"Sure I do, honey. Why do you ask?"

"I heard mommy say you're not a good agent."

His heart skipped a beat.

"She *told* you that?"

"No. I heard her talking on the phone." She looked up at him. "She also used a bad word."

———

Emily's night with Mike was even better than she had dreamed. They both took fast showers, then wore the bathrobes from her hotel room.

"I hope we're not doing anything wrong," Emily said.

"Why would you think that?" Mike said.

"I don't know. We're working together and—"

"So what? We're coworkers. I'm not your boss and you're not my boss. We can do whatever we want."

She smiled at him. "But I can be your boss for tonight." She kissed him on the mouth.

She noticed he wanted to take her robe off, but couldn't bring himself to do it, so she did it for him.

He drew her back, gently, and looked at her.

Naked.

His mouth opened as he said nothing.

"Well?" She smiled.

"Well what?" He blushed.

"Never mind." She walked up to him and took his robe off. She pushed him gently on the bed and started kissing his body, slowly. Then got on top of him. When he tried to cover them with the sheet, she took it off.

"I want to see you. And I want you to see me."

They made love twice, taking a nap in between.

The second time felt much better than the first.

———

After the conference ended, Emily checked out of her hotel room, and Mike asked her to stay for two more nights in his. She stayed with him and they spent most of the weekend in bed, with short breaks for gambling and food.

When they returned to New York on Sunday, they took an Uber to his apartment, and Emily stayed there for the night. His apartment was smaller than hers, but warm and cozy.

After a nap, they took the subway to Central Park and walked hand in hand for half a day, eating, talking, and sitting on the Great Lawn with a million other people. She put her head on his lap and he stroked her hair.

She forgot about work, bosses, and bad emails, and only enjoyed the sun, the trees, and the people around.

On Monday, they took the subway to work.

"I hope no one notices I'm wearing the same clothes as I did on the trip," she said.

"No one knows what you wore on the trip." He smiled.

She nodded as he kissed her in front of everyone on the subway.

"We need to play cool at the office," she said.

"You mean I'm embarrassing you?"

"No! But we don't need everyone in the office gossiping about us."

He nodded.

"Even though Jessica probably knows," she said.

"I still think you two set it up."

Emily tried to hide her smile.

That day Jessica looked at them with a weird grin. They kept their conversations short and work related.

"How did it go?" Jessica asked the first chance they were alone.

Emily smiled. "You know I'm not a girl who kisses and tells."

"You go, girl!"

Emily left the office fifteen minutes after Mike. They texted each other they would meet at the subway station. She was going to get her suitcase and go home, but ended up staying another night at his place.

————

The following morning, Emily found discrepancies in the company's earnings again.

"It should be only a hundred thousand dollars, not a million," she told Jessica in her office.

"Are you sure about that?" Jessica closed the door behind her.

"A hundred percent."

"How the hell do you remember?"

Emily put her laptop on the CEO's desk. "I know my numbers. That's my job."

Jessica swallowed. "Tell your boyfriend you'll be coming home late tonight."

"What?"

"We need to look into this." Jessica picked up her cell phone from her desk and walked to the door. "I'll be right back."

Emily went to Mike's office and told him she'd be staying late.

"Anything wrong?" It seemed as if he wanted to kiss her.

"Some discrepancies. I'm sure we'll find them soon enough."

She waited for Jessica for almost an hour. She texted her, then called her, but there was no reply. Emily went back to her office and reviewed the numbers again, for the seventh time.

After two hours, Emily decided she'd go home. She was the last one in the office, so she locked the door behind her.

"I thought we were working late tonight," Jessica said, startling her from behind.

"Jesus, you scared me." Emily caught her breath. "I've been waiting for hours. Where have you been?"

"I'm sorry. I had some important phone calls to make." Jessica unlocked the office and held the door open. "Shall we continue?"

Jessica locked the door behind them, and Emily followed her into her office.

The office was dark and deserted. If Jessica had been a man, Emily would have felt much less comfortable.

They checked the numbers, looking for earnings and expenses, and could not find where the error came from.

The number was exactly ten times as much as it should have been.

"I guess someone added a zero." Jessica grinned.

"Only you and I have access to this."

Jessica nodded. "Then it must have been you." She laughed, almost like a drunk.

"You know I don't make mistakes like that. I'd have caught it if it were me."

"I was kidding. It was probably me." Jessica seemed a few years older. "Let's erase it and go home."

———

Emily bought Chinese takeout and took an Uber to Mike's. They had dinner and she told him about the mistake she'd found.

"You must feel proud," he said.

"I do, but all these issues are starting to pile up. I'm starting to think something's going on."

"Probably mistakes." He kissed her. "It's a good thing we have you watching over our money."

"I don't know. I'm scared."

"Why don't you talk to Jessica? She's your friend. She'll tell you the truth.

———

Emily stopped by her apartment and dropped her suitcase from the trip. Then she took another Uber to Jessica's apartment.

"Who is it?" Jessica yelled from behind the door.

"Emily."

Jessica opened the door. "*Emily?* What's up?"

When she didn't reply, Jessica gestured for her to enter.

Even though they'd worked together for a long time, they'd never met in each other's apartments. Jessica's was much fancier than hers.

She makes more money than I do, but not that much.

"I'm sorry for the time and for not letting you know I was coming over, but I need to talk to you."

"No problem. What's up?"

"I couldn't talk to you at the office since I think it may be bugged."

"Why would it be bugged?"

Emily told her everything, while Jessica only listened and seemed surprised.

"Emily, I had no idea. I'm sorry about this. Why didn't you come to me sooner?"

"You had no idea?"

"No! What do you think I am? A mobster?"

Emily didn't reply.

"Why would I threaten *you*? You're my partner and my best employee. I wouldn't have gotten the company up and running without you."

Emily stared at her.

"Okay, look." Jessica opened her phone and scrolled through her emails. She opened the correspondence between them, where Emily had read the Reply All threat.

"See?" Jessica showed Emily her emails. "I didn't get that email."

Emily examined the phone, inhaled then exhaled.

"And for the rest of the problems we had—I didn't think it was any kind of corruption. I thought they were honest mistakes."

Jessica examined Emily. "Look, we always used to joke that our investor, Guy Cash, was a mobster—or something like that—but I never believed it. But who knows? Maybe he's part of it?"

Emily rubbed her thighs.

"Tell you what," Jessica said, "I have a friend who's a private investigator. Let me talk to him and ask him to check around, okay? Don't worry. I'll take care of it."

Emily tried to smile.

Jessica hugged her. "Now, let's have some wine, and you can tell me all about Mike."

———

A few hours later Emily took an Uber back to her apartment.

The next morning, Emily woke up screaming.

She found a dead rat next to her in bed.

PART 2
NEVER REPLY ALL

SIX

Emily waited until the weekend to talk to Mike.

"Someone's trying to shut me up," Emily told Mike in his apartment.

"What? What do you mean?"

She told him about the strange email and all the discrepancies she'd discovered.

"Who could it be?" He made her coffee.

"I don't know. Only Jessica knows about this. But why would she do that?"

"Because she's guilty? It wouldn't surprise me," he said.

"Really?"

"Yes. She's a bit of a sleaze-ball. You never noticed?"

Emily considered it. "I guess I have, but I always figured it was part of being a businesswoman. Especially in a man's world."

"Do you remember you were surprised to see the tech guy going out of your office?"

Emily nodded.

"Jessica let him in. She *must* be involved."

Emily stared at him. "Do you think she's stealing from the company?"

"Could be."

"What do we do?"

"You tried to talk to her but it didn't help. She kept pushing you away. I think it's time to go to the police or something."

Emily scratched her head. "There's an FBI agent who lives right next to me. I thought I should involve him."

"You trust him?"

"He seems like a good guy."

Mike nodded. "That could be a good idea."

He made them scrambled eggs and they sat down for breakfast.

"I never thought Jessica could kill a rat and put it in my bed," she said.

"Me neither. It scares me."

He got up and hugged her.

They finished their breakfast, made love, and took a nap together, naked in his bed.

"Be careful," he told her before she left.

————

Emily knocked on her neighbor's door before entering her apartment.

The agent's wife opened the door without asking who it was.

"Hi. I'm Emily, your next-door neighbor."

"I know who you are." She raised her eyebrows. "What can I do for you?"

"You're Lisa, right?" Emily remembered Bob had mentioned her name once.

"Yes. I'm sorry but I have something in the oven. How can I help you?"

"Sorry to bother you. But is your husband home?"

"No. Why?" She looked her up and down.

I have a boyfriend, Emily wanted to say.

Boyfriend. That sounds good.

She tried not to smile.

Lisa was older and, even without makeup, looked good.

"I wanted to ask him something."

Lisa raised her eyebrows again.

"It's...about his work. Do you know when he might be home?"

"He's at work, so God knows when he'll be back. I'll tell him you stopped by."

She closed the door.

———

Bob entered the apartment building after eight p.m. He knew Madison would be asleep, so he took his time talking to the doorman and checking the mail.

In the elevator, he saw an older woman who greeted him full-heartedly. He'd seen her in the past and always said hello.

She had a shopping cart full of grocery bags. When he held the door open for her to go out, it took her a long time to exit the elevator.

"Do you need help with that?" he asked.

She seemed as if she did, but she also seemed worried.

"Don't worry. I'm a federal agent." He hated doing that, but it seemed like a good cause. "And I also live right above you, on the fifth floor." He pointed up.

When he still seemed unsure, he showed her his badge.

She smiled. "I'd like that. Thank you, young man."

No one had called him a young man for a long time.

He helped her with the door and put the groceries in the refrigerator and cupboards, as she instructed him.

"Would you like a cup of tea?" she asked when he finished.

A beer would be nicer.

He looked at his watch. "I'm sorry. I need to get home."

She seemed as if she'd lost her best friend.

He looked around at her apartment, which seemed similar to theirs, but with old furniture. It didn't seem as if she'd had company in a while.

She seems lonelier than I am.

He looked at his watch again. "You know what? My daughter is probably already asleep, so I have time for a quick cup of tea." He smiled.

She smiled. "Won't your wife mind?"

He almost said *hell no*, but kept his mouth shut.

She nodded as if she understood. She went to the kitchen and put water in an old stove-top whistling kettle and put it on the burner she lit. He sat down and watched her make their tea, as slow as a turtle walking up a hill.

She told him about her husband who'd passed away a few years back, and how lonely she'd been since her children and grandchildren didn't come to visit enough. He told her a little about what he did at work, which seemed to impress her.

After he finished two cups of tea, he promised he'd be back to see her and left.

———

"Where have you been?" Lisa asked as he entered their apartment.

"Work. As usual."

"I saw your car in the parking lot over an hour ago."

Is she jealous? He tried not to smile.

"What were you doing in the parking lot?"

"I forgot something in the trunk."

He nodded. "I helped the old lady from the second floor." He put his gun away in the safe. "Are you jealous?"

She snorted. "The next-door neighbor came looking for you."

"Who? The weird young lady who lives across from us?"

"That's the one." She rolled her eyes.

"What did she want?"

"Don't know. Something about your job," she said.

Bob nodded.

"Maybe her phone got stolen and she thinks the FBI will track it down." Lisa laughed but her lips remained flat.

They kept silent for a while.

"She's too young for you," Lisa said.

"*What?* I don't...I hardly know her! We only say hi in the elevator. It's nothing like that. I—"

"Relax," Lisa said and turned to the bedroom. "I don't care."

———

The following morning, Bob knocked on his neighbor's door on his way to work. The neighbor seemed happy to see him and asked him in.

Bob looked back at his apartment, then nodded.

"Coffee?" she asked.

Bob had drunk one before he left, but when he saw she had a Nespresso machine, he couldn't say no to a cappuccino.

They drank their coffee in her living room. She was a fairly good-looking young woman. Ever since Lisa started talking about getting divorced, he wondered what it would be like to find another woman. He'd never seen a man come to her apartment, but even if he got divorced—Emily was too young for him.

She told him about herself, her work, and about moving to their apartment building.

Bob didn't share much. He didn't look for new friends, even though being out of his apartment felt good these days. And the coffee tasted good.

But he needed to get to work.

"I'm sorry but my wife said you needed something regarding my work?"

"Yes. I'm sorry." She fidgeted, then told him about the discrepancies she found at work. When she mentioned the dead rat, Bob opened his eyes wide.

He took out the notebook from his back pocket. He took notes and more details from Emily, and told her he'd look into it.

He asked to look around her apartment and she agreed.

"Did you give someone your keys?"

"No. Why?"

"I don't see any forced entry." Bob noted.

"Meanwhile, make sure you lock your door." Bob saw the cat sitting on the fridge and pointed at it. "Could it have killed the rat?"

"I doubt it. I just got him, and he's almost as small as the rat." Emily smiled. "I call him Romeo."

Bob nodded. "What did you do with the rat?"

"I put it in a bag and threw it in the building's garbage. And washed the sheets. Three times."

Bob shook his head.

"Stupid, huh?"

"A little. But don't worry about it. I can't promise you anything, but I'll see what I can do."

———

"It looks like he's taking it seriously," Emily told Mike on the phone.

"That's good. I'm glad. Do you want me to come over?"

"I don't think so. He said he might be back with a team or something."

Mike kept quiet.

"I mean I'd love to see you, but I think I need to see it through here. And you'll be safer in your apartment."

"You think you're not safe?"

"Bob...the agent, he said I should be careful."

"I'm worried about you."

"I know. I'll be fine. But thank you."

———

"You're not going to help her, are you?" Stuber asked Bob in his office.

"Well, she's my neighbor and she needs help—"

"She needs *the police*, not the FBI. And they probably won't do much about it either. We can't open a full-fledged investigation for anyone who comes to us for help."

"I did some preliminary investigation and realized this could help us in another case we're working on."

"*Really?* Which one?"

"Emily's start-up investor is *Guy Cash*. The one we're looking into for money laundering."

"Cash? You're kidding me."

———

Emily opened the door for Bob, who returned a few hours later with a small team. They weren't wearing FBI jackets as she'd expected. They seemed like regular people. They dusted for fingerprints and took a few pictures with a big camera. She took a picture of them on her iPhone when they didn't notice and wanted to send it to Mike. She wished she could post it on Facebook, but figured it wouldn't be a good idea.

Maybe it's not a good idea to send it to Mike, either? It might be illegal or something.

Bob asked a few more questions and took more notes in his small notebook.

Old school.

"We're looking into your company," Bob said. "And we'll need your help."

Emily nodded.

"You need to be careful, even though I'll try to keep an eye out. Call me if you see or hear anything suspicious. Even in the middle of the night. We'll install a camera next to your apartment. If someone comes back, we'll know."

"Don't they have cameras in the lobby?"

"Yes, but we couldn't find anything out of the ordinary that night. One camera didn't work. Whoever did this knew where the cameras were and knew how to avoid them."

———

Bob sat in his office with Agent Stuber.

"Are you sure you're not too involved in this?" Stuber asked.

"What do you mean?" Agent Bob said.

"With her being your neighbor and all."

"No." Bob clenched his teeth. "I didn't even know her before she approached me. She's a neighbor, but she's also a good lead into this company and someone who needs our help."

Stuber looked at his laptop. "She's not bad looking, either."

Bob stared at him with piercing eyes. He wanted to hit the table. "That has nothing to do with it."

Bob wondered if Stuber knew about his marital problems. He'd shared nothing at work, except with Craig, his best friend.

And his only friend.

Stuber would never be his friend.

Stuber got assigned to him after his last case went sour. He investigated someone who had threatened his family, which caused him to use more force than necessary to make the arrest.

Stuber was a young, arrogant agent. He thought he knew more than anyone else, which annoyed Bob. No one said it out loud, but he felt his bosses wanted Stuber to watch over him.

"Okay," Stuber said. "I looked into the company. You know more about this, but to me, it seems like a regular start-up. They got four million dollars total from investors. I read in an online article that the CEO bragged she'd received more than half of it only for a PowerPoint presentation. I still don't understand how people get money only for ideas."

That's why they don't put you in charge of sophisticated cases, Bob wanted to say out loud. *The best you can do is babysit me.*

Bob had been a co-founder in a start-up before he joined the FBI. It was a social media start-up which did well, but when it became obvious there was no point competing with Facebook, they had to shut down. Bob wanted to make a big change, so he joined the Bureau.

"It's a different economy. Investors have FOMO. Fear of Missing Out. They don't want to be the ones who gave up on the next Uber or Airbnb. In the past, it was easier to get funded if you had only an idea. Today they look more for traction."

"You mean they look for money coming into the company? Like a normal business?"

"Exactly."

Stuber nodded. "I guess that's why they pay you the big bucks."

Bob shook his head. "It's not easy anymore to get funded just for an idea. From what I saw online, the founder is impressive. Coded since an early age. She had a couple of start-ups as a teenager. What's their financial status?"

Stuber looked at his laptop. "The company has twelve employees, including your friend...your *neighbor,* and Jessica King, the founder and CEO. It looks like they have a profit. Not much, but something."

"No one with a criminal record?"

Stuber shook his head.

"Do we have access to their emails? Emily said she got a Reply All email which she believes threatened her."

"She didn't show you the email?"

"No, she said Jessica had let some unknown person into her office, and he deleted her email and all traces of it."

"Why would she need to access the office for that? She could have done it from the web, couldn't she?"

"Yes, but maybe they're low-tech, and—"

"Isn't it a high-tech company?"

"Not everyone knows how to hack a phone or an email account. Even if they work in a start-up company."

"Yes, but from what you say, I'm guessing Jessica could easily hack her computer."

"You're right. She could probably access all the employees' emails from a dashboard or something."

"Why didn't she erase it that way?"

"She may not be involved in this. For all we know, she could also be under threat."

"We need to talk to her."

"Yes, but not yet. I want to make sure she's not involved first."

"Okay, I'll work on getting access to their emails."

Bob nodded.

"Do you think Emily's life is in danger?"

"I'm not sure. I think they wanted to scare her to stop looking into the issues she found."

"If it were Jessica, she could have fired her."

"She could have, but that might make Emily want to get revenge. They probably think it's better to keep her close and keep track of her. This way they have legal access to her laptop and phone—which she got from work."

Stuber nodded. "What are we doing to keep her safe?"

"I've had a camera installed next to her apartment, on the pathway between our apartments."

A pathway which looked like a balcony connected to Bob's apartment. Emily's apartment was in the middle of the pathway, so when she opened the door she could see the outside. Bob's apartment was the first one after the balcony.

"An undercover agent will pass by the apartment every few hours," Bob continued. "I'll keep an eye out for her and her apartment as well. I don't think they know I live next door. They probably wouldn't have done this if they knew."

Bob read more about the start-up on his computer. "Do we have a list of investors, besides Guy Cash?"

Stuber checked his laptop. "Nope. He's the only one."

SEVEN

Emily and Mike went out to lunch alone. Usually, they'd have lunch with the whole company, but they both said they had things to do and couldn't get a break for lunch. Emily left first, saying she had a meeting, and Mike left fifteen minutes later, saying he'd get lunch with a friend.

Jessica smiled at her as if she knew.

Emily liked healthy food, so they met at a nearby *fresh&co* and stood in the long line with the rest of the New Yorkers. She would only eat junk food while traveling.

"What's here for a *man* to eat?" Mike asked after he kissed her.

She laughed. "Salad?"

"I don't eat that. That's my food's food."

"Sandwich?"

"Cheeseburger?"

"I don't think they have that here."

They sat at the only available table, which only fit two people, and was bolted to the floor adjacent to the wall. Next to them sat another couple, lucky enough to get a table for four. Even though the other couple had much more room than Mike and Emily, they sat less than two feet from them.

Too close.

"What happened with the FBI?" Mike asked as she chewed on her salad.

Emily looked around. Even though the couple next to them didn't seem to be paying attention, she kept her voice low. "My neighbor—the agent—came and asked me questions, said they'll investigate. He sent a team to check for fingerprints and—"

"*Really?*" Mike said aloud. "Like in the movies! I didn't think they did that."

"Shhh." She gestured for him to lower his voice and looked around. At second glance, the couple next to them seemed like tourists.

She thought they may not speak English, but she couldn't be sure since they didn't speak to each other at all.

The place was still packed with people working in the area and maybe a few tourists. She looked around until she noticed a mustached man sitting alone. He wore blue jeans and a T-shirt and only drank a soda. He could pass for a thirsty, lonely tourist—but he stared right at her.

"Are you okay?" Mike held her hand. "Maybe you shouldn't be there alone, maybe you should—"

"Shhh." She told him again, eyes still on the lonely man, who had dark hair and a mustache.

"What's wrong?"

"Don't look now"—she tried to hide her mouth—"but I think someone is watching me." She played with her food. "Watching *us*."

"*What?*" He jumped in his seat.

Exactly what she didn't want him to do.

Emily lowered him back to his seat with her hand. The man saw Mike jump but moved his eyes elsewhere.

"Let's not talk about this here." She lowered her voice. "Tell me something about work."

Mike spoke but Emily's eyes were glued to the mustached man who didn't look at them again. A minute later, he rose and walked casually outside.

When Emily couldn't see him anymore, she looked back at Mike, whose mouth was open wide.

"You haven't heard a word I've said, have you?" he asked.

"I'm sorry. That guy freaked me out."

He followed Emily's gaze.

"He left," she said.

Mike sighed. "As I started saying before, I'm worried about you. You shouldn't go back to your apartment."

"Nonsense. They installed a camera next to my apartment. I have the FBI neighbor watching me. He also said an undercover agent will come and go."

"Okay." He nodded slowly. "If you're sure."

"Besides, where else would I go?"

"You could stay with me."

It was her turn to open her mouth wide.

———

As Bob watched the footage from the camera in front of Emily's apartment from a few days back, Stuber entered his office without knocking.

"She wasn't lying," Stuber said and sat across from him.

"Please knock next time." Bob raised his eyes from his computer screen. "Who?"

"Your neighbor." He waved a piece of paper in his

hand. "I got a reply from Google. They sent me the email she thought she saw. She was right."

Bob took the paper and read the email.

"That could count as a threat."

"Should we pick her up?"

"Not yet." Bob read the email again. "It only says 'Get rid of her.' It can also mean *fire her*." Bob eyed Stuber. "I also want more evidence on the CEO first. I'll tighten the security around Emily's apartment."

Stuber seemed like he had something to say, but didn't speak.

Bob returned to the footage on his computer as Stuber left. Because of the proximity of their apartments, he could see everyone who came and went from his own apartment as well. He saw himself going out early in the morning. He fast-forwarded to see his wife and daughter leave together to go to kindergarten. He smiled as he saw Madison, who seemed happy to go. He thought she enjoyed going there, but rarely took her there himself.

She hadn't wanted to leave his or Lisa's arms the first few days they dropped her off, and after they'd leave, they could hear her still crying inside.

It broke his heart each time, even though he knew she needed time to adjust.

Two hours later in the video footage, he saw his neighbor, Emily, going out to work.

He forgot how late they started working in high-tech.

As Emily locked her door, she searched around. When she noticed the camera, she smiled and went out of view.

Bob fast-forwarded to when his wife and daughter returned. He smiled when he saw them, but also felt an ache in his stomach. He froze the video and zoomed in on his wife.

She looked as beautiful as she'd been when they first met.

He didn't want to divorce her.

But he knew she was right. He was married to his work.

Should I quit?

He considered it every now and then. Every couple of weeks. Every time he missed something Madison did. Every night he didn't get a chance to be with his wife. Every time his life was in danger.

Is it too late now? She seems serious. She wants me out.

Would she reconsider if I quit my job?

He held his phone and stared at her name on the contact list. It felt like asking a girl out for the first time.

It took him a long time to text her, *Hey. How about dinner tonight?*

He could see she read his message but didn't respond.

We can still have dinner together. We're still married, he thought.

Technically.

Stuber stormed into his office without knocking.

Bob minimized the video.

"You won't believe what I found," Stuber said.

Bob stared at him.

"I read in an online interview where Jessica said the Cash guy gave her a million dollars."

"So?"

"I checked their bank records. They only transferred half a million."

Bob looked at the paper he'd handed him. "Why do you print everything? Isn't that what old people do? Can't you think of the environment?"

Stuber waved his hand.

Bob studied the paper. Cash had transferred half a

million dollars four years earlier. A year later the investor transferred an additional half a million dollars. He showed it to Stuber.

"The interview was right after the first half a million was transferred," Stuber said.

"Maybe she got it wrong," Bob said. "Or maybe the CEO knew she was supposed to get more money, and it slipped out before it got wired. It's customary for investors to give money in chunks after milestones are reached."

Stuber threw another piece of paper on his desk. Bob picked it up.

"A few days after the second transfer, the CEO gave a statement she'd received *another* half a million. It means she *said* one and a half million when we can see a transfer of only one million dollars."

Bob stared at him.

"I think Mr. Cash is not called Mr. Cash for nothing."

EIGHT

Emily spent the day staring at her computer. She didn't have much work, and she could only think of what Mike had said during lunch.

"You could stay with me," he'd said.

Are we taking our relationship up a notch, or is he worried about me?

Or both?

She had stayed with him, but only on a long—a very long—date. He'd never invited her to stay.

When he passed next to her office, he saw her through the glass and smiled.

She smiled back and pointed at the phone in his hands.

He raised his palms.

She picked up her phone and texted him.

When he saw the message, he smiled.

I'd love to accept your offer, she'd texted him.

———

Emily left food and water for Romeo, packed a small suitcase, and took the subway to Mike's apartment. She texted Bob that she'd be out of her apartment that weekend, and Bob thanked her for letting him know.

Mike greeted her with a warm smile and let her in. There were two champagne glasses on the table.

After a while, she asked to be excused and went to the bathroom. She returned wearing a new sexy black lace nightgown.

It had been a long time since she'd worn one of those.

His jaw dropped. "Is that new?"

"Yup. Got it today."

"For *me*?"

"No, for my next-door neighbor."

"The FBI agent? He's not bad looking, but he's a bit old—"

"You idiot!" She pushed him to the couch and remained standing. "Even though he needs a new woman."

"What do you mean?" He laid on the couch looking up at her.

"Never mind about that now. I got this as a thank you gift. For *you*."

He grabbed her gently and lowered her to him. She sat on top of him, knees bent, then bent over for a kiss.

When he took off her nightgown, she said, "What a waste of thirty bucks."

"It wasn't a waste," he said, examining her body.

They made love in the living room, then had dinner, then made love again in his bed.

"You said something about the agent needing a new woman?" He stroked her hair.

Emily had returned late from work one night and saw

Bob's wife walk past the doorman in a hurry, holding a man's hand. At first, Emily thought it was Bob and walked up to say hi, but when she almost caught up to them she noticed it was another man.

Emily stopped short and hid in the mailroom. She didn't want to make Lisa feel uncomfortable.

She considered telling Bob, especially now when he was helping her. She thought she should tell him, but also figured it wasn't her business.

Also, it might make him mad.

"I saw his wife bringing another man home one night."

"What?" He pulled back. "Are you sure it wasn't a handyman or something?"

"It was late at night and they were holding hands."

"Wow." He touched his mouth. "They did it right in front of you?"

"No. I came home right behind them. They didn't notice me."

"That's sad," he said.

"It is. Marriage sucks."

He drew back. "What do you mean?"

"I mean it's hard. People can't stay together for too long."

He looked away.

She touched his hair.

"You mean that?" He looked at her. "You don't want to get married?"

"I'll be honest and say I didn't ever see myself marrying. But if a special man came along—I might change my mind."

"Do you think you'll ever find one?"

"Hmmm...I don't know. Do you have someone in mind?"

He pinched her thigh.

"Ouch!" She laughed, hit him, then kissed him.

———

They planned on going to Central Park or a museum but ended up in Mike's apartment for the rest of the weekend. They shared their time between his bed and the couch— binge-watching shows on Netflix.

———

"I had a great weekend." She stood over his bed early Monday morning.

"Indeed." He pulled her in for a kiss.

"I need to stop by my apartment."

"So early? We don't need to go to work for another three hours."

"Are you ready to go to work together?"

"You're right. You go first."

"You know, I could stay a little longer, and not go to my apartment."

"Where will you leave your suitcase?"

She looked around. "Here?"

He smiled and pulled her back to bed.

———

"We don't have enough for a warrant to tap them or search their offices," Bob said to Stuber in his office.

"Why the hell not?"

"All circumstantial. We can't prove anything."

"What about the threat in the email?"

"Not enough. It could also mean fire her, and that's still legal."

"Damn it!" Stuber hit Bob's desk. When Bob stared at him, he didn't even apologize.

"Calm down," Bob said. "We'll keep track of them. They'll make another mistake soon."

NINE

If you don't let it go, what happens to him will be your fault, a text from an unknown number appeared on Emily's phone.

She sat alone in her office, staring at her phone. Mike had left early for a family matter, and Jessica had left for meetings.

"What should I do?" Emily said into her empty office. She rose and started pacing. "I should talk to Bob."

Her phone dinged again. Another text message, reading: *And don't involve the FBI. We'll know.*

"What the hell?" she said, but put her hand over her mouth as if to shut herself up.

She started looking around the office.

Is someone bugging my office? Are they listening to me?

There had been a guy in her office, she knew that for sure. He'd erased her email, but had he done anything else? Could he have planted a bug?

Jessica had access to her office, as did the cleaning guy.

What do I do?

She wanted to call Mike, but if someone had bugged her office, it may not be a good idea.

She sent him a text message. *Is everything okay?*

It is, he replied immediately. *I miss you. Are you home yet?*

Not yet. Wrapping things up. I'll talk to you later.

She stared at a selfie they took together in Las Vegas.

I can't lose him.

I just got him.

He's too good for me.

Do I tell Bob? Or do I handle it myself?

———

Bob met Craig in a bar one evening after work.

They hugged and sat down for a beer.

"She's hot," Craig said, pointing at a woman sitting by herself on the other side of the bar.

"Do you need a wingman?" Bob laughed.

"Nah. I never did. But *you* do."

"*Me?* I'm married. You're single. Go get her."

Craig rubbed his neck. "From what you tell me, not for long."

Bob sighed. "I still hope things change. I'm even considering leaving the Bureau for her."

"Really?" Craig almost rose.

"This work ruined my life. Ruined my marriage."

"But the Bureau *is* your life. You won't be able to live without it." Craig took a sip from his beer. "That's why I never got married."

"I've decided to leave."

"Are you serious? Are you sure it'll help? It may be too late."

"If you're here to cheer me up, you're not doing a very good job."

"I'm sorry. I'm trying to be realistic." Craig rubbed Bob's shoulder. "I don't want you to be left alone *and* without a job."

Craig had a point.

Should I do the hard thing and quit to prove to her she's more important? Or should I see if I get her back, then quit?

They were quiet for a while until Craig asked about Stuber.

"I hate him. He keeps annoying me. I don't know what to do about him. I feel like he's babysitting me."

"He probably is, but there's nothing you can do. You should lay low and let it pass."

Bob shook his head.

Craig knew about Bob's previous bad encounter. In an earlier case, Bob arrested a suspect who screamed at him he would kill his wife and daughter. Bob had no idea how the suspect knew so much about him and threw him to the ground, grinding his face in the dirt before his partner pulled him off. The FBI suspended Bob for a few days, and after a hearing, they let him go back to work, with a warning. Stuber joined him and made him feel like he's keeping an eye out on him.

The man was a frequent resident of the local jail and had been arrested many times before for resisting arrest and threatening violence against officials and their families, so no one cared Bob had hurt him.

"It shouldn't have happened, and it will never happen again," Bob had told his supervisor in the hearing.

"It'll pass," Craig said, interrupting Bob's thoughts.

"It's another reason I want to quit. Work has become almost unbearable."

"I know. I'm sorry," Craig said. "How's the case you're working on?"

"That's not going so well, either. We can't get enough for a warrant. And it doesn't seem to be going anywhere."

"I hate those cases. I understand it's your friend?"

"A neighbor. They scared her, but I'm not sure I can help."

"*Her?*"

"Oh, enough with that. She's a young woman. A neighbor. That's it."

"Okay. Sure." Craig finished his beer and got another one.

Bob didn't get another beer. He didn't like to drink more than one bottle when he had his gun on him. They watched the Yankees play on one of the big screens at the bar.

Craig had a few beers, so Bob walked him to his apartment, not far from the bar. They hugged goodbye and promised to meet again soon.

———

A few days later, Bob watched the footage of his neighbor's apartment again. He chose to view only when motion was captured on the camera, deciding the technology was good enough, so he could spend less time watching the videos.

The sound of thunder startled him.

He looked back at the screen and saw Emily come and go. She mentioned a new boyfriend from work, but he'd never seen him.

Maybe they broke up?

Or was she afraid to bring him to her place?

He saw himself leave early and return late. He also saw Lisa and Madison come and go a few times.

The only strange thing he saw was a big man coming late one night, stopping next to Emily's place, and using his cell phone. The man stood with his back to the camera and seemed suspicious.

Bingo! We got someone. As soon as he turns, we'll have a good video.

But the man didn't use any kind of disguise, which seemed odd.

Bob wanted to call Stuber, but after taking a closer look at the man, something about him—his size, his shape, his walk—seemed familiar.

Too familiar.

It couldn't be.

Could it?

Bob rubbed his neck.

What the hell was Craig doing there? Is it possible he had anything to do with Emily? Was he checking on Bob's case?

Maybe it wasn't Craig?

Or maybe he came to visit me one night, and I didn't know about it?

But Craig never showed up at my apartment.

What the hell?

Bob looked closer as his apartment door opened. His wife, Lisa, stood there in her nightgown and smiled at the man who appeared to be Craig.

Bob didn't understand at first. Or maybe he didn't want to understand.

But when she kissed his best friend on his doorstep—Bob's mouth went dry and his stomach clenched.

When she let him inside and closed the door while kissing him passionately—Bob picked up the picture of his wife from his desk and flung it across the room, smashing it against the wall.

PART 3
END OF WATCH

TEN

Lisa met her best friend Olivia in a coffee shop in Manhattan after dropping off Madison at kindergarten.

They hugged and discussed their jobs. Lisa did part-time fashion consulting for a retail chain store but hated every minute.

"How are things with Bob?" Olivia asked.

Lisa sighed. "I told him."

"About Craig?"

"No! Are you crazy? I told him I want a divorce."

Olivia shook her head. "How did he take it?"

"Not well."

"I can imagine. He still loves you."

"I know. But it's not enough." Lisa bit her index finger-nail. "I can't stand being alone anymore."

"I understand. Are you absolutely sure about this?"

"No. But I've decided it has to be done."

Olivia nodded. "And what about Craig? Do you love *him*?"

"I don't know. But he's fun. I like the excitement."

"Excitement doesn't last. A man like Bob...does."

"You think I'm making a mistake?"

"You know I do."

Lisa's eyes filled with tears.

"He's a good guy," Olivia said.

"I know. But I'm too mad at him. I've been alone most of the time since we got married."

Olivia opened her mouth to say something, but Lisa said, "And don't tell me he's saving the world and all that shit. I need a man with me, not a man who cares about the rest of the world more than me."

"He doesn't." Olivia leaned away from her. "I must tell you, this doesn't sound like the Lisa I know."

Lisa stared blankly at the wall behind Olivia. After a while, she burst out crying.

Olivia asked for a glass of water and held her hand.

"I don't know what happened to me either." Lisa wiped her tears and exhaled. "I grew up without a father since he was always away on business. My mom hated him for it. When I grew up, I understood he was screwing around. I promised myself I'd never have a husband like him."

"Bob isn't like that! I know him. He'd never screw around."

"You're probably right, but it got the best of me." Lisa rubbed her face. "I don't know how I got myself into this mess. I was so angry with him I couldn't control it."

"It's not too late to fix this. You can talk to him. Try to patch things up." Olivia drew back. "And get rid of Craig."

Lisa took a long sip of water. "You're right. I know you're right."

"Will you tell him about Craig?"

"Are you crazy? He'll kill him. He'll kill us both."

Emily couldn't decide if she should go home or go to Mike's apartment.

She decided not to get the agent involved. *Not yet.* It seemed they knew what she was doing, and until she figured out how they did it, she would do what they say.

She wanted to see him. She wanted to make sure he was okay.

If something happened to him, it would be my fault.

She paced back and forth in her office, then thought they might have cameras there as well. She searched inside the light fixtures, on the shelves, and the smoke detectors. She couldn't find anything, but, with today's technology, it was probably too hard to spot a tiny camera.

She couldn't stay there anymore.

She left the office and took the elevator down to the street. She searched but couldn't see anyone who seemed to be following her.

Would I even notice if someone did?

I'm only a computer geek.

But she'd read some spy novels.

She should go to Mike. She entered the subway she usually took to her apartment, then got out at her usual station. She went back into the station from another entrance, then took a different train to his place.

In case someone's following me.

She got off the train a station before she should have and walked the rest of the way. When she got to his apartment, she knocked on his door.

After a few minutes, she knocked again.

And again.

But Mike didn't answer.

—

Bob stared at his screen and couldn't believe what he'd seen. He wiped the tears from his eyes and looked at the broken glass from Lisa's picture on the floor.

When someone knocked on his door he screamed, "Not now!"

He returned to his screen and watched the short clip again and again. He wanted to believe it wasn't Craig.

He wanted to believe it wasn't Lisa.

But there they were.

Sneaking around behind my back.

Fucking.

My two best friends in the world.

Bob checked the timestamp on the video.

It had happened one night after Craig met Bob at the bar.

One night before Bob told him he wanted Lisa back.

Craig told him to move on. Bob thought it was a friendly word of advice.

But it wasn't.

Craig tried to persuade me to let her go.

The son of a bitch! Bob slammed the desk with his hand.

When he watched the next clip, nearly two hours later, he saw the door open and his wife kissed the man again at the doorstep.

Lisa seemed happy and in love.

Craig walked in front of the camera now, facing it for the first time. Bob had hoped it wasn't him, but when he saw his face the tiny hope evaporated.

He'd wanted to be wrong.

They'd been fucking for two hours.

In my bed.

While my daughter slept in the next room.

Seven minutes after Craig left, Bob saw his own back coming into view.

They'd missed each other on the elevator.

Craig, or Lisa, knew exactly when Bob would get back home.

Bob remembered Lisa had seemed asleep that night. Like she did most nights when he got home.

Or she pretended to be.

Bob rewound the recording to where he could see Craig's face again. He wanted to point his gun at Craig's head, maybe even pull the trigger.

The man who set them up also broke them apart.

———

Stuber burst into Bob's office.

"I'm sorry—" Stuber stared at him, then looked at the broken glass on the floor. "Is everything okay?"

Bob wiped his eyes and yelled, "Why are you bursting into my office?"

Stuber shook his head. "Bob, we got the fingerprint analysis from Emily's apartment."

I don't care, Bob wanted to say.

"So?"

"We found Jessica's fingerprints there."

"So?"

"I read your notes from your interview with her," Stuber said. "Emily said Jessica had never been to her apartment."

ELEVEN

"Mike!" Emily yelled as she knocked on his door.

Then she screamed his name.

Then called his cell phone.

But no one replied.

She texted him *Where are you?*

She knocked again, and when some neighbors passed by and looked at her strangely, she asked them if they'd seen Mike.

They hadn't.

He didn't reply to any of her knocks, calls, or texts.

She sat at his doorstep, her head between her hands.

After an hour, she called Bob.

But the FBI agent didn't answer her either.

———

"Get a warrant to search Jessica's apartment and office," Bob told Stuber. "I'll be back in an hour."

"Where are you going?" Stuber said, but Bob passed him on his way out of the office without saying a word.

Bob parked next to Craig's apartment and knocked on his door. Hard.

When no one replied, he contemplated calling him.

"Bob?" A voice came from behind him. "What are you doing here?"

Bob wanted to reach for his gun.

"I need to talk to you."

"Sure thing." Craig reached for his keys. "Come in."

As they entered his apartment, Craig gestured for him to sit.

"Is everything okay?"

Bob shook his head.

"Coffee? Tea? Beer?"

Bob shook his head.

"What's wrong?"

Bob rose and walked back and forth in the apartment.

"Is anything wrong with Madison? Or Lisa?"

Bob raised his head and stared at him. His teeth clenched as hard as he could without breaking them.

"You son of a bitch!"

"What?"

"You're screwing my wife!"

"*What?*" Craig almost lost his balance. "Are you crazy, Bob? What are you talking about?"

"Do you think I'm an idiot?"

"No!" Craig rubbed his neck. "Why would I be with your wife? I set you guys up."

"That didn't stop you."

"Bob, you're talking crazy. Is Lisa having an affair?"

Bob nodded.

"And you think it's someone you know?"

Bob stared at him.

"Don't try to play me. I know those techniques."

Craig nodded, sat down, then rose.

"You guys are getting a divorce, so technically—"

Bob took a swing at Craig, striking him on his right cheek. The blow knocked him back, and he fell to the floor.

Craig reached for his gun but didn't pull it, his face pale, besides a red cheek. "Bob, what the fuck?"

Bob pulled out his phone and saw his neighbor's name.

It could be something important.

He ignored the call and flipped to the video on his phone.

He'd sent the surveillance video to his phone and showed it to Craig.

Craig's mouth opened wide as he saw himself and Bob's wife kissing at his best friend's doorstep.

———

After calling Agent Bob a few times, with no reply, Emily's phone rang.

Mike!

"Mike? Thank God! I was worried about you! Where are you? Are you okay? I'm here—"

A man answered instead. "We have him. He's safe for now. But you have to do what we tell you."

———

"Bob, I don't know what to do. I'm sorry. I didn't mean for it to happen. I swear."

Craig sat up on the floor. Bob sat in front of him.

"How *did* it happen?"

Craig lowered his head.

"I asked—"

"Are you sure you want to hear?"

Bob nodded.

"Does she know you know?"

Bob shook his head.

"She came to the office one day. You were out on an assignment. She wanted to talk, so we went out for a beer."

Bob closed his eyes. He imagined her looking for him, then going down two floors to Craig's office. He imagined her telling him she needed to talk. He tried to shake the image of Lisa and Craig walking outside the office together.

And the image of them kissing.

And the image of them fu—

"We had a few beers. She told me how hard it was for her, that you're never home, and one thing led to another." Craig lowered his eyes. "I'm sorry."

"How could you do this to me?"

Craig didn't reply.

"You are...you were my best friend."

Bob's phone rang again. He glanced at it and saw it was Emily again.

He switched the phone to silent and let it go to voicemail.

"Call her now and tell her it's over," Bob said.

Craig opened his mouth, then closed it. After a while, he asked, "What do you mean?"

"You need to end this. *Now*."

"Bob. You guys are getting a divorce. She doesn't want you anymore. Don't you get it?"

Bob drew his gun and aimed it at his best friend's face.

———

Emily stopped calling Bob after ten failed attempts. The agent was ignoring her or was doing something more important.

They sent her a text with instructions. She would meet their contact in her apartment. The contact would tell her what he needed from her.

That's good. Bob could see the man entering my apartment on the video surveillance.

Maybe that's why he didn't pick up. Maybe that's why he's busy.

The man told her not to talk to the Feds, but if the Feds saw the bad guy and came looking—she could do nothing to prevent that.

Emily imagined the FBI storming her apartment, guns drawn, arresting the bad man.

The instructions they gave her were to get to her apartment in thirty minutes.

She figured a taxi would be the quickest. When she checked her Waze app, she figured she might not get there on time.

I'm in a taxi. I may be a few minutes late, she texted whoever had Mike's phone. *Please don't hurt him.*

A reply arrived a few minutes later.

We will if you're late.

TWELVE

Bob saw his ex-best friend through his handgun's sights.

"Put the gun down," Craig shouted at Bob. "Are you crazy?"

Bob lowered his gun slowly, but still aimed it in Craig's general direction.

If Craig pulled his gun on him, it would be self-defense. *Could I really shoot him?*

"Bob! What are you doing? You're not a murderer! You can't kill me over something like this. Don't be crazy."

Bob put his gun on the table, the barrel still pointed in Craig's direction. They both stared at each other for a long time.

———

Emily used the line she'd heard in movies a million times, but never thought she'd use herself. "I'll give you an extra twenty if you make it fast."

The driver smiled and did what he could in the New York traffic.

She tried to call Bob again.

After the taxi stopped next to her apartment building, she ran up the stairs to the fifth floor.

As she reached her apartment, she checked her watch.

She was thirty seconds late.

———

Craig's cell phone rang, startling Bob.

They both stared at it.

"Should I get it? It could be important."

Bob kept staring at the phone.

Then Craig's home line rang, which startled them both.

"Who still has a landline?" Bob gazed at the phone.

"I'm taking this. It could be important."

Bob didn't reply. Craig got up and walked to the phone, his eyes glued to Bob.

"Craig here," he said into the phone. "Yes. He's here." Craig stared at Bob while listening. "Okay. We'll go there now."

Craig hung up. "Put your stupid gun back in your holster. Your partner was looking for you but you didn't answer. He traced your phone here. He said an armed man broke into your neighbor's apartment."

———

Emily took out her keys and tried to open the door.

But it was jammed.

She looked at the camera, then at Bob's door.

No sign of him anywhere.

What do I do?

The door swung open and a strong arm pulled her in forcefully.

———

Bob jumped into Craig's car. Craig drove into the streets, sirens blaring.

Driving fast in New York during rush hour was almost impossible.

Bob checked his phone and saw both Emily and Stuber had called him multiple times.

"I'll have to report you," Craig said.

Bob stared at him, nodded, then called Stuber.

"What's going on?" Stuber said. "I've been trying to reach you for a long time."

"I had issues with my phone. Since when do you trace my phone?"

"I didn't. I'll explain later," Stuber said. "About thirty minutes ago four people entered Emily's apartment. It took the surveillance guy some time to see it, understand something was wrong, and report it. I saw the footage. I could recognize two of them: the CEO and Emily's boyfriend. It seemed as if they were forcing him inside. It could be a kidnapping situation."

"What do they want with the boyfriend?" Bob asked but didn't wait for a reply. "SWAT on the way?"

"Yes. A little while later, Emily showed up, tried to open her door, and someone pulled her into the apartment."

"Damn. We'll be there soon. Traffic is hell. Where are you?"

"I'm out of town. Tomorrow is my day off. But I'm on my way there."

"Okay. I'll have NYPD evacuate the building." He

checked his watch. "Thank God my wife and daughter are in dance class."

Stuber fell silent.

"I'll call you when I get there."

"Bob?"

"What?"

"I'm sorry, but Lisa and Madison entered your apartment right after Emily got to hers."

———

Emily stumbled and fell to the ground. When she looked up she saw Jessica, two unfamiliar men with guns, and the man she loved.

"Mike!" Emily tried to get up but stumbled. "Are you okay?" She reached for him but one of the men pushed her hand away forcefully.

Mike nodded.

"*Jessica?* Are you behind all of this?" Emily looked up at her.

"I'm sorry, Emily, but I have a company to take care of."

"You call this taking care?"

"A CEO's gotta do what a CEO's gotta do." Jessica stuck her thumbs in her pockets.

Jessica had always liked the power position she was in. Once, she even showed Emily a special business card she'd made that read *I'M CEO, Bitch,* like the one Mark Zuckerberg had when he was young.

Was it more politically correct for a woman CEO?

"Kidnapping your VP of Marketing is part of that?" Emily rose and wiped her pants clean.

"Nah. That's collateral damage. We needed to make

sure you'd cooperate. I thought the rat would be enough, but you didn't get the hint."

Emily swallowed. She searched for Romeo and saw him in his usual spot, on top of the refrigerator.

There's nothing he can do to help, but at least he's safe.
Maybe I should get a dog next time?

She'd learned karate when she was a child, but hadn't practiced it much in recent years. Could she use her instincts to do something? Or would it be stupid to try?

"You got me. Now let him go."

Today was all about quoting clichés from movies.

In the movies, the man usually asked the bad guys to let his woman go.

Chauvinistic pigs.

"Sure. After we get what we came for."

"What *did* you come for?"

Jessica laughed.

"First thing's first. Does your boyfriend know you wanted to go with him to the conference in Vegas, just so you could dump him later?"

Jessica's laugh turned wild.

"What?" Mike asked.

"You're lying. She's lying, Mike. She set it up. I never asked her to do it. And I never had plans to dump—"

"Yeah, right," Jessica said. "I needed you two to get together, so I could keep an eye on both of you. I knew I should have never had such a good CFO. You do nothing but count my money all day and cry when there's a nickel missing."

"What?"

"To be honest? I never needed a CFO. Who needs a CFO in a start-up? It never occurred to you as odd?"

"*What?*"

"Never mind," Jessica said. "I need you to give me the files you stole and I'll be out of here. You won't have a job, but you'll get to keep your life, and his."

Emily had wanted to get to the truth and knew it could cost her her job.

But now her job seemed less important.

"What files?" Emily asked.

"You think I'm that stupid, huh?" Jessica said. "I know you took the Excel files home with you. You uploaded them to Dropbox and then deleted them. I knew you wouldn't be fooled easily so I had to keep track of you. But you weren't smart enough to do it without leaving a trace."

Emily stared at her. "The guy you let in to spy on my computer?"

"Nah. He only deleted the stupid email you got." Jessica rubbed her hands. "I sent him there knowing you'd see him. I thought you'd figure you were in danger and stop snooping around, but you didn't. You know I can access your work computer legally. That's how I know you deleted the files. But I also know you have the Excel files on your laptop."

"My personal laptop? How the hell do you know what I have on there?"

Jessica smirked. "I'll tell you the truth. I had some nice spyware planted on your laptop without you knowing."

"You what?" Emily yelled. "You were never anywhere near my laptop."

"You remember the charging cable you borrowed from me? The one I told you you could keep?" She didn't wait for a reply. "It had a chip on it, and it let me hack your laptop." She laughed. "You can't trust anyone with anything these days."

Emily wanted to punch her.

"Especially not your CEO," Jessica said.

"I should have known."

"You should have."

"If you had access to my laptop, why didn't you delete the file?"

"I did. But that's how I know you were lying," Jessica said. "And now I need the files and anything electronic you may have, including passwords and everything."

Why is she giving me so much information? Is she planning to kill us after we give her everything?

Where the hell is the FBI?

"I don't have them. I deleted them right after you said I had it wrong."

Jessica shook her head, then gestured to one of the men.

The man grabbed Mike and pushed his head toward Emily's table forcefully.

Emily screamed and ran toward him.

But the other man, who seemed prepared, extended his leg and Emily fell. When she got up, the man punched her back to the ground.

Mike screamed.

————

Bob called his wife, but she didn't pick up.

If bullets started flying, they could penetrate their apartment.

They could hit Madison.

Oh, my God!

On the fourth try, Lisa answered.

"Lisa! Why didn't you pick up? I need you to take Madison and leave the apartment right now."

"Bob? What are you talking about?"

"Lisa, please don't argue, just do it. There's a...situation next door. A dangerous one. Take Madison and leave now!"

He realized it was the first time he'd spoken to her since he heard about Craig. Should he say something?

It didn't matter now.

He felt Craig's eyes on him.

"Lisa?" Bob said.

"Okay. Okay. We're leaving."

————

"If you deleted the files from my laptop, you know they're gone," Emily said.

"You think I'm stupid, huh?" Jessica said. "I know you kept a copy on a flash drive."

Emily's face turned white. "How do you know that?"

"The spyware, remember?"

It was worth a shot.

"We also know you tried to call the FBI on your way here," Jessica said.

"No, I didn't. You told me not to."

"We have your phone tapped. Stop lying!" Jessica yelled.

"Now give me your phone, your laptop, and any other electronic device you have."

Emily shook her head.

"No problem." Jessica gestured to the man holding Mike.

He took out a pair of grass shears from his pocket and forced Mike's finger into it as Emily screamed.

————

"Leave the phone on," Bob said.

He heard Lisa talk to Madison, explaining they had to go. When he heard the door open, he asked her if she could see anything suspicious.

When she said no, he remembered the last time he'd seen their apartment door. On video.

He heard her close the door.

"I hear a woman screaming!" she told Bob.

"Shit!" Bob yelled. "Run as fast as you can. We'll be there in a few minutes. The police are there already. Leave now!"

Then he heard a woman's voice next to his wife. They exchanged a few words Bob couldn't understand.

The line went dead.

THIRTEEN

Emily heard noises from next door.

Maybe the agent came home?

Should I yell?

Jessica heard the noises as well. She shushed Mike and gestured for the man closest to the door to check it out.

He peered through the peephole, then looked back.

"Woman with a child," he whispered.

"No agent?" Jessica asked.

How did they know about the agent?

The man shook his head.

"Maybe we should use them to get to the agent, in case he decides to show up?" Jessica said, almost to herself, and walked to the door.

"Wait!" Emily said as Jessica touched the door handle. "Think about it. You won't be able to get away with it. They'll hunt you down. It's not a couple of start-up employees, it's an agent's wife and daughter. You can't kill them too."

"Something's wrong!" Bob yelled. "I can't get her back. Step on it!"

He should have told them to wait and hide in the apartment. He hated himself for that mistake.

He called the agent watching the surveillance camera outside his apartment. "What do you see?"

"A woman stepped out of the apartment and is talking to your wife."

"Is my daughter there?"

"Yes, sir."

Bob swallowed.

"Is she doing anything to them?"

"No. They're talking."

"Oh God. Send me her picture and keep me posted." After a few seconds of silence, he asked, "What's going on?"

"Nothing so far, sir. Still talking."

He knew Lisa. She wouldn't go down without a fight. She'd give her life to protect their daughter.

He couldn't bear the thought of living without them.

Even after what she did to him.

———

"Miss, I need you to go back to your apartment please," Emily heard Jessica say. "There's a police matter here."

"Police? My husband is with the FBI. I heard screams. What's going on?"

"Miss, we're interrogating a suspect. Please go back or I'll have to arrest you."

Emily tried to peer outside but couldn't see them.

When the other man with the gun started walking toward the door, Emily yelled, "Lisa, run! They have guns! Run and get Bob!"

The man turned to Emily and hit her on the head.

Jessica looked back, only for a second, then stepped out. She grabbed Madison and pulled her into the apartment, causing Lisa to go in with her. Jessica did something outside and came back in.

"What the hell's going on?" Lisa yelled.

"Don't worry, they'll come to get us soon," Emily said.

"It'll be too late," Jessica said, and pulled a gun.

———

"The woman is pulling your daughter into the apartment!" the agent yelled to Bob over the phone. "Lisa followed after her."

Bob's mouth dried up and he clenched his seat.

"What now?" Bob yelled.

"She came out. She's...she did something to the camera! I have no visual!"

"Tell the SWAT team to move in," Bob screamed. "Now!"

———

Emily grabbed an ashtray she'd never used from her coffee table and threw it at Jessica. She missed, but it made Jessica look back.

Lisa kicked Jessica in the groin, grabbed Madison, and sprang outside of the apartment.

Jessica fired at the door.

Emily and Mike screamed.

———

Craig parked the car next to Bob's apartment building. Police cars surrounded the place. Officers were escorting people out of the building.

He sprang out but Craig grabbed him.

"Let SWAT do their work!"

Bob saw SWAT getting ready nearby.

He hated when, in the movies, the agent or detective would lead the SWAT team into a high-risk entry. The investigator, usually unprotected so the audience could recognize him, would never go in front of the extremely shielded and trained team.

It irritated him.

It was hard to stand there and do nothing, but he knew Craig was right. The SWAT team would do the best work possible.

Craig was probably worried as well. Maybe as much as he was.

But then Bob heard a gunshot.

FOURTEEN

With a rush of adrenaline, Emily stormed at the man holding Mike down. She grabbed his hand and pulled the grass shears out of his grip.

Jessica, who'd opened the door and started going after Lisa, looked back and decided to return.

Emily and Mike wrestled with the man, and as he tried to pull the grass shears away from them, they stuck it into the man's stomach.

The man fell into a fetal position, holding his stomach, screaming.

"Run to my bedroom and lock the door!" she screamed at Mike.

He stared at her for a second, then grabbed her hand and started running to the bedroom.

Jessica shot in their direction as Mike was the first to enter the bedroom.

———

Bob couldn't wait for SWAT, so he started running into the open back door of the apartment building, where the last people were being escorted outside by police officers. Craig yelled to him as two uniformed police officers grabbed Bob.

"I'm FBI! Let me go."

They let him go, and he stormed in.

Craig followed him.

They ran up the stairs to the fifth floor, pushed the door open, and ran toward the apartment.

Bob couldn't see Lisa or his daughter anywhere. When he reached his neighbor's door, he saw two bullet holes in the door.

"Lisa!" He screamed and kicked the door in.

———

Lisa grabbed Madison, who was crying, and ran back to their apartment. On the pathway to their apartment, she almost slipped, but regained her balance and sprang to their door.

She closed the door and tried to open Bob's safe.

He should have a spare gun there.

But she didn't know the code.

Then she heard gunshots.

———

Emily saw Jessica running toward her bedroom as someone kicked down the door. Jessica turned and fired at the man in a suit holding a gun.

She recognized her neighbor, Agent Bob.

Emily closed the bedroom door with Mike in it.

It wasn't his problem.

Bob screamed and fell back. Emily grabbed Jessica and struggled with her to the floor.

Someone she'd never seen before—maybe another agent —stormed in and fired at the man closest to the door.

The second agent missed, so the man grabbed him and wrestled him to the floor.

———

Bob ignored the sharp pain to his left arm. He'd not stormed the place as he should have, but his mind wasn't working straight. He had to find his wife and daughter, and nothing could stop him.

He rose to his feet as Craig entered the apartment, shooting someone, but missed. Bob scanned the apartment. Craig wrestled the man while Emily fought her boss, Jessica. A second man lay on the floor in a pool of blood, facing away, holding his belly screaming.

No one else seemed to be in the apartment.

He aimed the gun at the man wrestling Craig, then at Jessica.

"Lisa!" He screamed and started sweeping the apartment.

"She ran away," Emily yelled from under Jessica. "With your kid. I think they're fine."

Bob returned, eyes blank. He yelled for them to freeze, but no one did.

He aimed the gun at the man wrestling Craig. If he shot, he'd risk shooting Craig.

But Craig wasn't innocent.

Craig fucked his wife.

No one knew Bob knew.

If he shot Craig by mistake, no one would suspect him.

FIFTEEN

Agent Stuber arrived at the scene as the SWAT team was ready to storm in. He'd gotten an update from an NYPD officer, who told him Bob and Craig stormed alone into the building.

"As far as we know, we evacuated everyone from the building, except the other agent's wife, daughter, and their neighbor."

Stuber nodded, dressed up in a Kevlar vest and a helmet, and hurried the SWAT team to go in, trailing behind them.

As they all climbed up the stairs and got ready to storm the apartment, Stuber worried less for Lisa and the child, and more about Bob doing something stupid.

———

Bob had Craig and the man he wrestled with in his gunsight when the man got hold of a knife from his pocket and raised it to Craig's head.

Bob fired three shots and everything went quiet.

A few seconds later, the sound of grenades rushed through the air, as all the people who were still alive in the apartment started coughing hard.

––––––

The SWAT team entered the apartment, yelling at everyone to lie down. No one resisted, and after they hand-cuffed everyone, they continued their sweep and brought Mike out of the bedroom, handcuffed.

Emily smiled when she saw him walking on his own two feet.

––––––

Stuber entered the apartment as the agent in charge after SWAT cleared it. He recognized Emily and Jessica, both handcuffed on the floor.

He saw Bob on the floor next to them.

"Tell them to let me go," Bob said.

Stuber nodded but didn't. Instead, he walked over to another man, lying dead on the floor with bullet holes in his head. Next to him lay Bob's previous partner, blood on his forehead.

Stuber leaned next to Craig and touched him.

"What happened?"

"He tried to kill me with a knife," Craig said, "and Bob shot him dead."

Stuber nodded, then told SWAT to release the two agents.

SIXTEEN

"You knew Craig was having an affair with my wife?" Bob asked Stuber in his hospital room.

Stuber nodded.

"How?"

"I saw the video."

"But I erased it."

"I saw it before you did."

Bob nodded slowly. "Did you make a copy?"

Stuber shook his head.

"When you entered the apartment with the SWAT team, you thought I'd killed him, didn't you?"

Stuber stared at him, then nodded.

"I thought you knew me better."

Stuber shrugged. "Good thing I was wrong."

Bob suffered a small injury to his arm and was supposed to get released a few days later. His wife had run back to their apartment, locked the door, and hid in their bedroom with Madison.

They were safe.

Emily and Mike were treated for minor injuries and released.

Jessica and the man who was left alive were locked up, awaiting trial.

"Is Jessica talking?" Bob asked.

"Yup."

"Do we know who the two men who helped her in the apartment were?" Bob asked.

"She said they were just hired help. They knew nothing."

"Was Mike in on it with her?"

"She didn't say."

"Did she say who wrote the initial email? The one that got this whole thing started?"

Stuber nodded. "She said it came from Cash. But she said he only wanted to—what's that phrase you use?"

"Defraud investors?"

"That's the one," Stuber said. "But Jessica only wanted to get more cash—*cash money*—for herself. Seems like the company wasn't doing as well as we thought."

"All of this craziness for money?" Bob exhaled.

"People do crazy things for money."

Bob nodded.

"I still don't know what *defraud investors* means."

Bob smiled. "I thought she wanted to overstate the company's revenues so that investors would invest in the company at a higher value. I guess that's what Cash wanted, but I'm not sure we can prove it."

"At least Jessica will go to jail for a long time."

Bob nodded. "Now we have to get Cash. Somehow."

———

A few days later, Mr. Cash summoned Emily to Jessica's office.

"Quite a story you had," he said.

Emily had met him a few times but didn't know him well. At first, she thought the threatening email came from him, but after Jessica was in jail, the FBI blamed it all on the CEO.

Emily hoped she entered the shortlist to replace Jessica. She had enough brains, talent, and knowledge. She also knew Mike was on the same list.

She would be happy for him if he got it.

"We need to find a new CEO," Mr. Cash said. "Both you and Mike were on the shortlist."

Were?

They made up their minds?

Emily moved in her seat.

"Who do you think is better?"

"I think we're both good. We both have experience, knowledge, and the ability to run the company. I learned a lot from Jessica. Well, from the good things she did. And this company needs to be led by another woman."

Mr. Cash nodded. "We picked Mike. After what happened, we feel you can't be a part of this company. You can take your stuff and leave."

When Emily left the office, Mike didn't look at her.

He knew.

They had probably told him before they told her.

She took her belongings from her office, and when she passed Mike, she asked him to call her that evening.

But he never did.

EPILOGUE

Stuber and Craig entered Bob's hospital room and sat next to him.

"We have some updates," Stuber said as Craig waited behind him, almost out of sight. "Cash fired Emily and promoted Mike to be CEO."

"*Really?* I thought he'd keep Emily as CEO," Bob said. "I even suspected at one point that Emily had something to do with things so she could be CEO."

"No. Not Emily."

"What do you mean?"

"We still have a bugging device in Jessica's office. I'm not sure it's admissible in court, but this is what we picked up."

Stuber launched an app on his phone and put it in front of Bob to listen.

"We trust you," Bob heard Cash say. "You'll do a better job than Jessica. For sure."

"Yes, sir," Mike said from Stuber's phone.

"I knew you'd be a good fit to spy on both of them," Cash said. "I didn't think you'd take it as far as you did, but it worked."

"I couldn't get to Jessica this way, so I figured getting close to Emily would be good enough."

"I had no idea Jessica was so crazy."

"Me neither," Mike said. "What are we going to do with *Emily*?"

"I have no use for her anymore."

They both laughed.

———

After Stuber left, Craig sat on the only chair in Bob's hospital room. They both kept quiet for a long time.

"I ended things with your...with Lisa," Craig said without looking at him. "I'm sorry again for what happened. I don't know how, or why..."

Bob looked away.

"To be honest," Craig said, "*she* broke up with me."

Bob stared at him.

In the video, she seemed like she was really into him. What happened?

Does she want me back?

Is there a way I could take her back?

"Did you report me?" Bob asked.

Craig stared at him, but after a moment shook his head.

"Are you going to?"

Craig raised his eyebrows. "You could have killed me in that apartment."

Bob nodded.

"Why didn't you?"

"I'm not a murderer." Bob squinted. "I'll be honest and say I wanted to, but that's not me."

After a while, Craig rose. "You're a good agent. And a

good man. I'm sorry again for what I did. There's no excuse."

Craig left and Bob bit the inside of his cheek.

Craig never said he wouldn't report him.

THE END

Author's note

If you've enjoyed *Never Reply All*, please check out the next book in the series—***Don't Dare to Dream***.

Agent Bob will return later in the book, but in the meantime, you can get to know David, Rick, and Angela, who have a unique and crazy story. The book starts a little slower, but the suspense builds up to an explosion...

You can get it here:
www.amazon.com/dp/B07KDW2TBN

Stay in touch

Please subscribe to my mailing list on my website to stay in touch:
www.danfriedmanauthor.com

PLEASE LEAVE A REVIEW

If you've enjoyed this book, it would be great if you could leave a review.

Reviews help me bring my books to the attention of other readers who may enjoy them as well.

To leave a review:
www.amazon.com/product-reviews/Bo7ZRJ4CXN

Thank you!

ACKNOWLEDGMENTS

Many people helped me with this book, and I hope I haven't forgotten anyone.

People who read and suffered through first drafts of the book, and helped me improve it immensely: my teacher, mentor, and editor William Berndhardt, my wife Avital Friedman, my brother Sharon Friedman, and Melissa Ammons.

Even though the book is more FBI than the police, the people who helped me with this part were my dear cousin, Sergeant Dekel Levy, and my friend and a fellow author Sergeant Brandon Watkins. I'd also like to thank Retired Police Captain Dave Cobb. All the mistakes and inaccuracies are mine. Stay safe, guys.

As usual, the Internet was a great help as well.

TURN THE PAGE FOR AN EXCERPT

A brilliant has-been entrepreneur gets a chance for a new life, only to discover it was a part of a big scam. If he doesn't return the stolen money, his life might be over.

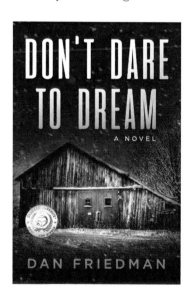

ONE

David held his breath as he watched the pickup truck storm toward a woman and her little girl about to step into the crossroad.

The woman steered the red Target cart out of the store using her elbows, eyes glued to her phone. The girl, wearing a pink dress and a matching hair bow, strolled behind her.

The pickup truck driver eyeballed his phone.

David had only wanted to get snacks for dinner, but what happened next felt like a scene in slow motion; he saw the driver blow through the stop sign, and with a force only God could explain, he ran, grabbed the girl, and tried to finish crossing the road.

He had not run in over ten years.

The pickup truck screeched to a halt a few inches from them.

David exhaled slowly and tried to smile at the girl, but she was crying for her mother.

The next thing he knew, someone was helping him sit on one of the red concrete balls in front of the store while a man offered him water. People gathered around him, staring. Someone pulled his arm and asked if he was okay. A woman squatted in front of him, her hand over her mouth.

He thought he heard someone somewhere say the word *hero*.

Every inch of his body ached. His heart raced as he gasped for air. The little girl stared at him from her crying mother's arms. She hugged her mother and inspected the crowd around David. When the crowd dispersed, the mother bent over him, hugged him tight for a few seconds, and kissed his cheek.

Some of her tears wet his face.

"Thank you, sir. Thank you so much."

He tried to smile.

Almost dying was worth the hug and the kiss.

Too bad she was probably married.

———

Rick MacMillan sat in his new Chevrolet Camaro in front of Target and couldn't believe what he had just seen.

TWO

David drove up to the black gate at the entrance to his apartment complex and pushed the remote a few times until it opened. The stupid thing worked randomly, and when it did, it took ages for the gate to open.

The management had installed the gates following a few burglaries. They wanted the tenants to feel secure but never offered actual statistics. The gate was like putting a Band-Aid on a broken skull—anyone could wait for a tenant to open the gate and drive in after them.

David tried to feel good about saving the little girl's life, but his body ached from the short run. He'd pulled every muscle in both legs. He wondered if he'd really moved that quickly. Maybe it just felt that way.

A sidewalk separated the car from his apartment, which kept him from parking even closer. He lifted a foot to climb it, but his legs couldn't hold his weight and he tumbled backward, missing his car by an inch. He crashed to the ground, his head hitting last, and he felt as though he'd made a dent in the pavement.

He tried, but failed, to push himself up. After a few tries, he decided to wait for someone to help him.

But what if no one came? Maybe I should call 911.

That would be embarrassing.

He thought of the old commercial: *I've fallen and I can't get up.* He was too young for that.

He fumbled for his iPhone, but it took him a few minutes to roll his wide body over and get it out. As he tried to overcome his blurred vision, a man kneeled down next to him and grabbed his arm. "Are you okay, buddy? What happened?"

Where the hell did he come from?

David had met Rick last week, when the tall, handsome neighbor from upstairs came knocking on his door. Rick was at least a head taller than David and wore a tight T-shirt, which emphasized his muscular physique. His body seemed as if it could burst out of his shirt.

Rick said he'd scratched David's car while moving his furniture in and insisted on reimbursing him, despite David's protests that the car was old and that he didn't intend to repaint it.

Rick was standing in his way of getting his daily dose of junk food, so David had to wave him off.

Now, as he lay in the parking lot looking blankly up at Rick, he thought having a friendly neighbor wasn't so bad after all.

"I'm fine. Thanks," David whispered.

Rick's eyebrows rose. "Let me at least help you up."

Rick dropped a gym bag from his shoulder and tugged at David, his big muscles flexing under his shirt, but he was too heavy even for Rick. It took a joint effort to get David to his knees and then for him to sit on the curb.

Rick looked at him. "Do you need an ambulance?"

David shook his head. He hated doctors.

Rick retrieved his bag, pulled out a bottle of water, and handed it to David.

After David took a few sips, Rick helped him up and walked him into his apartment, gripping his arm until David settled in his recliner.

Rick examined the apartment. "Would you like me to call someone?"

David stared up at him from his recliner, then shook his head and gazed at the ceiling.

"Is there anything I can get you?"

David shook his head.

"Would you like me to stay for a few minutes?" Rick asked, but David had already dozed off.

———

Rick watched David sleeping in the recliner.

He sighed. *This man needs to change his life. It's a wonder he's still alive.*

He went to the kitchen and saw a sink full of dirty dishes. He inspected the unopened mail on the counter—medical bills, bank statements, junk mail.

He moved to the bedroom and saw an unmade queen-size bed without a frame. He doubted the fatso's bed saw any action. A single brown plastic nightstand stood next to the bed with an old night lamp and a phone charger on it. A small desk with a printer covered with dust filled the corner of the room, dirty clothes scattered on the chair next to it. He opened the nightstand drawer, but a noise from the living room startled him. He closed the drawer, sprang to the bathroom, and flushed the toilet. When he returned to the living room, David was still sleeping.

Rick sat for a few minutes, then returned to the night-stand drawer. He feared a sex toy jumping out at him, but instead saw an old iPhone, earphones, and batteries.

He returned to the living room and stared at David. Rick shook his head and slipped his hands into his front pockets.

————

David opened his eyes and saw a man in his bedroom.

What the hell is he doing there? Is this a dream?

He dozed off again. When he awoke, a man lay on his couch a few feet from him, reading from a phone. David wanted to speak, but his tongue was too heavy. He gazed at the man.

"You're up?" Rick dropped his feet to the floor and sat up.

David said nothing, so Rick continued: "It's me. Rick. Your neighbor. You fell outside, and I helped you into your apartment. How are you feeling, buddy?"

"You're still here?" David asked.

"I hope it's okay. I didn't think I could leave you like this." Rick rose, bent over to look at him, imitating a doctor, then sat back down. "Are you feeling better?"

David stared at him.

"You want me to take you to a hospital or call an ambulance? I'm kinda worried."

David shook his head. After a moment, he said, "Why are you still here?"

"I didn't go to med school, but I looked it up online"—Rick held his phone up—"and saw you might've gotten a concussion. I didn't want to leave you alone like this. I almost called an ambulance a few minutes ago. Are you sure you're okay?"

David nodded.

"Do you want me to go?"

David nodded again. "I'm sorry. I want to be alone."

Rick rose and straightened his shirt. "Sure. I have a meeting I have to go to anyway. I'll leave you my card. Don't hesitate to call me if you need anything."

"Thank you," he whispered.

As Rick turned the doorknob to leave, David asked, "Did you go into my bedroom?"

You can read the rest here:

www.amazon.com/dp/B07KDW2TBN

ABOUT THE AUTHOR

Award-winning author Dan Friedman likes to write thrillers where regular people deal with extraordinary situations.

Dan is also an editor and an entrepreneur. He has an MBA, and in the past, he was a technology journalist and a programmer. Dan lives with his wife, two children, and their dog.

His debut novel Don't Dare to Dream won the 2019 Reader's Favorite Gold Medal Mystery Book Award!

For more information:

www.danfriedmanauthor.com
dan@danfriedmanauthor.com

facebook.com/danfriedmanauthor
bookbub.com/authors/dan-friedman
amazon.com/Dan-Friedman/e/B07KDWZ95G
instagram.com/danfriedmanauthor
twitter.com/danfr

Made in United States
Cleveland, OH
13 March 2025

15134713R20076